☑ **W9-BFN-129**

Praise for
RECKLESS
⌐ and ⌐
The Amanda Roberts series

"A beguiling tale of love and murder deep in the backwoods of Georgia. . . . Good romantic suspense is hard to find these days. Sherryl Woods hits the spot with this dandy debut."
—*Rave Reviews*

"FOUR STARS! *Reckless* is a treat almost as good as a chocolate soufflé, but without the calories. Enjoy!"
—*Inside Books*

"Believable, appealing and immensely entertaining, Amanda Roberts is a woman of today."
—*Mystery News*

more. . .

"Particularly wonderful is the mix of Southerners invaded by some Northern folks . . . realistic characters are captivating while she advances us through a suspenseful, sometimes humorous, whodunit."
—*Mystery News* on *Ties That Bind*

————◆————

SHERRYL WOODS has published over forty novels since 1982 and has sold over four million books worldwide. She has written six Amanda Roberts mysteries and she received the *Romantic Times* award for Best New Author of Romantic Suspense in 1988. A former real-life news reporter in the South, very much like her highly praised fictional sleuth Amanda Roberts, Sherryl Woods now lives in Key Biscayne, Florida.

————◆————

Also by Sherryl Woods

Hide and Seek
Bank on It
Ties That Bind
Stolen Moments
Body and Soul

Published by
Warner Books

Sherryl Woods

Reckless

WARNER BOOKS

A Time Warner Company

To Paul and Dorothy,
Who'll always hold the winning ticket
when it comes to friendship.
with thanks and love

Warner Books Edition

Copyright © 1989 by Sherryl Woods
All rights reserved.

Cover design by Jackie Merri Meyer
Cover photo by Herman Estevez

Warner Books, Inc.
1271 Avenue of the Americas
New York, N.Y. 10020

 A Time Warner Company

Printed in the United States of America

First Printing: February, 1989
Reissued: December, 1993
10 9 8 7 6 5 4 3 2

CHAPTER

One

THE first thing that struck Amanda as she stood in the midst of the suddenly hushed crowd was that debonair Chef Maurice would not have chosen this way to die—facedown in a warm chocolate soufflé. The chef's hat he'd worn at a rakish angle was askew, its pristine white streaked with chocolate. The dirty mixing bowls, which he'd scattered about with a flamboyant disregard for neatness, were in broken bits on the floor and his utensils were scattered about like so many stainless steel pickup sticks. It was not, as they say, a pretty sight.

There was very little question that Chef Maurice was dead, even though Linda Sue Jenkins, the receptionist at the local veterinary clinic, gave them all an instant's hope. She ran up and, after lowering him to the floor of the makeshift stage, tried valiantly to administer artificial respiration. When she finally sat back on her heels and shook her head, a collective sigh went up from the

—1—

crowd. Looking stunned and oblivious to her own state of disarray, Linda Sue dabbed ineffectually at the chocolate stains on Maurice's clothes as if she, too, knew how horrified the elegant chef would be by the mess.

Suddenly the activity in the cookware department on the third floor of the recently renovated Johnson and Watkins Superstore seemed to slow before Amanda's eyes. The first gasps of dismay came singly and then in a mounting chorus. The fascinated stares of the onlookers appeared frozen in place, and the familiar whir of the automatic shutter on Larry Carter's Nikon whined on as he captured the scene from every angle for her newspaper's next edition.

It took a shrill scream and the distinct buzz of hysteria to shock her into becoming participant, rather than observer. She ran to the nearest pay phone and, after a guilt-ridden instant of indecision, called the sheriff's office first and then her editor.

"I knew you'd love covering that cooking demonstration, once you got into the spirit of it," *Gazette* editor Oscar Cates barked when he heard her breathless voice. Amanda clenched her teeth.

Amanda had worked for tough editors, obnoxious editors, alcoholic editors, and brilliant editors who could fine-tune a story, snipping out the excess with the precision of a skilled plastic surgeon. She had never before worked for a man like Oscar and, God willing, she never would again. If Oscar had had any notion that his crummy little feature assignment was going to turn into front page news, he'd have been here himself, leaving Amanda in the office to write yet another breezy roundup of quilting circle activities.

It was not every day that a world-famous French chef keeled over during a department store cooking demonstration. It would be big news almost anywhere, but Amanda guessed that in this particular section of rural Georgia it was probably the biggest story since McDonald's opened a franchise and gave away free soft drinks to the first 100 customers.

"Forget the cooking demonstration," she retorted. "I've got a better story."

"Dammit, Amanda, I sent you over there to watch that chef what's-his-name . . ."

"Maurice."

"Yeah, that's the one. You're supposed to give me ten inches of copy on how all the ladies in the crowd are swooning over the guy."

"They're swooning all right. The man is dead."

She heard the two front legs of Oscar's chair hit the floor with a resounding thud and figured she had his full attention at last. Deep in his heart, Oscar had always wanted to work for one of those lurid national tabloids. The location of his birth, an untimely but apparently satisfactory marriage, and a general lack of ambition had kept him tied to Georgia and a weekly paper that required no more than half his attention. Still, the thought of what he could make of this news had obviously stirred the watered-down printer's ink in his blood.

"What the hell happened? Did he choke on a Georgia peach pit?"

"You should only be so lucky," she retorted, picturing Oscar's sensational headline over that story:

DEMONSTRATION IS THE PITS FOR DEAD CHEF

The very thought of it made her shudder. "We don't know what happened," she said before Oscar could get any wild ideas. "He hasn't been examined by a doctor and the sheriff's not even here yet."

"What's the sheriff got to do with it? You don't think this guy's death was a murder, do you?"

Amanda had run across a few corpses during her stint on the police beat in New York. She'd learned to detect the clues that separated a death from natural causes from one in which the victim had been helped along. Even without a knife sticking out of his back or a bullet wound in his head, Chef Maurice had all the symptoms of the latter. The telltale blue beneath his fingernails, the vacant stare, and dilated pupils practically spelled cyanide poisoning. She had a feeling if she'd gotten close enough, there would have been a convincing odor of burned almonds on his breath as well.

Still, she demurred from making a judgment. "I'm no coroner."

"Maybe not, but according to the clips in that fancy résumé of yours, you've seen your share of stiffs. What's your best guess?"

"That Chef Maurice is dead."

"Okay, forget it," Oscar grumbled. "Wait for the coroner's ruling. Just don't blow your deadline."

"Oscar, we work for a weekly. The deadline is four days from now. I'm not likely to blow it, unless the sheriff's on one of his fishing vacations again and we have to wait for him to get back from communing with nature."

"The sheriff owns the damn store. He's probably in his office counting his money. Just take the escalator down to that fancy executive suite there and drag him back to give you some quotes."

"I think this is one case that will require help from the Atlanta police before the sheriff decides to talk. It's a little bigger than catching a speeder out on Route twenty-nine. Even Bobby Ray's not likely to blow it by making premature statements."

"Don't go getting snide about this town with me, gal. Is Larry getting pictures?"

"Of course. Got to run, Oscar," she said before he could offer any of his less than sage advice on how to work this story.

Amanda Roberts had grown up in Manhattan, she'd gotten her journalism degree from Columbia and her law degree from Harvard, and she'd had every intention of building a career as one of the best investigative reporters in the country. She'd been well on her way to doing just that until her husband, Mack Roberts, had gotten an offer for a full professorship in economics at the University of Georgia in Athens. For a man whose avocation was the Civil War, it had been the opportunity of a lifetime.

Mack had insisted on settling a few miles away in a town so small it didn't even have a supermarket, much less a movie theater. You had to drive ten miles to a 7-11 just for a loaf of bread, even farther if you wanted something fancy like a greeting card or, heaven forbid, a pair of jeans that didn't have Wrangler stitched on the back pocket. In fact, this store was the only one between Atlanta and Athens to actually boast enough floors to require an escalator. Kids came over on the weekends just to ride it.

Anyway, Mack had wanted the peace and quiet and quaint small-town atmosphere. Neither of them had counted on the fact that roosters crowing at dawn were every bit as noisy as the average New York traffic jam.

"Give it a try," he'd pleaded and, because she'd loved him and knew how important it could be to his academic career, she'd agreed.

"One year," she vowed, "and if my brain begins to atrophy, we go someplace else."

Unfortunately, it had been Mack's brain that had apparently suffered some kind of mid-life hardening of the arteries because he'd fallen in love with a nineteen-year-old sophomore about twenty minutes after their arrival. It had taken him slightly longer to get around to mentioning it to Amanda.

By the time Mack had asked for a divorce, Amanda was working on the only paper in a fifty-mile radius that wasn't intimidated by her credentials. Oscar, in fact, wasn't even vaguely impressed. He had her covering shopping mall dedications and ice cream socials over a three-county area, instead of corruption in government, corporate insider trading, or organized crime. Exposés, even if Oscar had been willing to share them with her, were in short supply. In fact, there hadn't even been a shooting in town, unless you counted the morning a hung over and testy Seth Henry had blasted his rooster with a shotgun for crowing at dawn. Frankly, Amanda had sympathized with him.

Still, if one of her job applications to papers in New York, Washington, or Los Angeles didn't pan out soon, she might seriously consider planting tobacco or peanuts or something—although the drooping, yellowing leaves of the plants she and Mack had received as housewarming presents did not bode well for that career either.

Today, however, was definitely looking up. Not for Chef Maurice, of course, but for Amanda it had turned unexpectedly into the most challenging assignment she'd had in months. Popping one of her favorite, special-order gourmet jelly beans into her mouth, she went back to start interviewing the witnesses: an assortment of store employees, adoring fans, and people who'd gotten caught up in the excitement when they'd stopped by to pick up one of the electric can openers on sale for $7.99, a one-day special that apparently held the same allure here as Macy's storewide bargain days back home.

Scanning the crowd, she spotted a woman who was sitting on the edge of the makeshift stage, a handkerchief pressed to her quivering lips, her eyes red-rimmed from crying. Amanda approached slowly, put her hand gently on the woman's shoulder, and asked if she could help.

The woman shook her head, not taking her eyes from Chef Maurice's body, which someone had covered with an incongruously bright blanket from the linen department two aisles over.

"It's all my fault," the woman murmured. "I should have done something to stop it."

Amanda's journalistic antenna quivered. She was not, however, a sneaky reporter. She did not believe in getting a poor vulnerable woman like this one to open up, only to tell her later that she'd just spilled her guts to a journalist. Before the woman could say another word, Amanda introduced herself and sat down next to her, noting with some surprise that the woman was wearing an unexpectedly stylish and expensive Norma Kamali ensemble, Ferragamo pumps, and a store ID tag with her name on it: Sarah Robbins.

"Why do you think this is your fault, Sarah?" Amanda asked, wondering if the woman's tears were predicated on nothing more than the certain knowledge that this disaster might mean the end of visits by cookbook celebrities? Because the woman was, in fact, shedding tears profusely, she thought it might be rather cruel to bring up her suspicions.

"I'm the manager of this department. It was my idea to get Chef Maurice to come here after that chocolate lover's event in Atlanta. I pleaded with his PR people for weeks," Sarah said between sobs. "Oh, how I wish they hadn't given in."

"Are there any people traveling with Chef Maurice?"

Sarah nodded, twisting the handkerchief nervously. "His public relations manager is here. He went down to get the limousine ready. The chef had to make a very tight plane connection from Atlanta. He was supposed to leave the minute he'd served the soufflé. We'd . . . we'd promised to end on time, but not . . ." She choked back another sob. "Not this way."

Amanda patted her hand. "Then the manager doesn't know yet?"

"I don't think so. He hasn't come back up."

"What's his name?"

"Jonathan Webster." She lifted her tear-streaked face.

"He's going to be heartbroken. He and Chef Maurice were very close."

Amanda wasn't so sure about that. It was her experience that public relations people were no more fond of their clients on a personal level than, say, criminal defense lawyers were. She was not about to disillusion an innocent like Sarah Robbins on this point, however.

"Will you be okay?" she asked. "I'll go and try to find this Mr. Webster."

"Yes, please. That would be very kind. He's wearing one of those unconstructed linen jackets, beige I think, and a hot pink T-shirt, probably a Ralph Lauren. Oh, and no socks. I noticed that right away. Not many men in this area go around without socks. He must watch the reruns of 'Miami Vice.'"

Amanda found Jonathan Webster as he was about to step onto the escalator. She identified him by his bare ankles and a T-shirt that would, no doubt, fit in quite nicely in an art deco hotel on Miami Beach. His hair was styled, not simply cut by some barber whose idea of a trim was to leave you looking like a marine recruit.

"Mr. Webster, I'm Amanda Roberts. I must speak to you."

"Sorry, lady," he said brusquely. "Chef Maurice doesn't do autographs."

"Not anymore," she muttered under her breath, as she stepped onto the escalator and climbed rapidly to the step behind Jonathan Webster. She had to elbow three excited kids out of the way to accomplish the feat. "I'm not looking for an autograph. Actually I'm a reporter. Sarah Robbins, the manager of the cookware department, sent me to find you. There's a bit of a problem. The chef . . ."

She hesitated, searching for a compassionate way to break the news just in case Sarah had been right and these two men had been friends. She toyed with several euphemisms such as "passed on" and "gone to his reward," and finally settled for being straightforward: "Chef Maurice is dead."

She watched Jonathan Webster's handsome face very closely for his reaction. She'd anticipated a wide variety of possibilities, but laughter hadn't been among them. Jonathan Webster howled until tears ran down his tanned cheeks.

"Lady, you sure do have a unique approach. What is it you want? An interview? Is that it? You deserve one for getting my attention like that. I like a woman with spunk."

Spunk? Amanda decided on the spot that she didn't much like Jonathan Webster. Unfortunately, the man held the key to a great deal of information she might need. "I'm sorry. I'm not joking, Mr. Webster. Your client died moments ago. The police are on their way now."

Webster turned absolutely pale at last and stumbled as the escalator reached the top and tossed him out on the third floor. His eyes darted to the chaotic scene before him and confirmed Amanda's words. "Oh, my God," he breathed softly. "Oh, hell!"

"Would you mind telling me a little about your client?" Amanda persisted doggedly, but Jonathan Webster was already making his way toward the stage. Just before he got there he squared his shoulders and tried to put some of the jauntiness back in his step. For sheer bravado, it wasn't a bad performance.

Still, it was evident that it was going to be awhile before Mr. Webster would be in any shape to do an interview. Amanda began circulating through the crowd again, asking questions, jotting down names.

Now that the first rush of horror had died down, there was a buzz of excitement in the air. Most of the people were milling around, talking to their neighbors. None seemed in any hurry to leave. Amanda picked the next group to approach, but just as she took her first step toward them a man bumped into her, spilling a tiny paper cup of water down the front of her blouse.

"Oh, dear," he said, flushing with embarrassment. He pulled a neatly folded handkerchief from the pocket of his gray suit and tried to dab at the stain.

"Please. It's okay. It was only water."

"But your lovely blouse."

"It will dry," she said with a smile. "Do you work here?"

"Oh, no. I just stopped by to pick up one of those can openers for the wife. She was feeling a little under the weather with this heat or she would have come herself." He held out a hand. "Henry Wentworth."

"Amanda Roberts. So, Mr. Wentworth, were you here when this happened?"

He nodded, his eyes suddenly drawn toward the stage. He shoved his hands in his pockets.

"I got here just as he keeled over. Who is this guy?"

"He is—well, he was—one of the hottest chefs in the country. Haven't you ever seen him on TV?"

"I guess not, but then I don't watch much except

those 'National Geographic' specials. The wife probably knows who he is. What do you suppose happened?"

"The police will have to decide that. Are you sure you didn't see anything that struck you as being a little odd?"

He blinked and stared hard at her. "I told you I just got here. Who are you anyway? A cop?"

"No. I thought I'd explained that. I'm a reporter."

"That's just as bad. I got nothing more to say. Sorry about your blouse."

Amanda shrugged and moved on. She headed for a heavyset woman who was bracing herself against a display of cookware and waving one of those flat, Teflon-coated frying pans in front of her face to create a breeze. "Terrible. It's just terrible," she said, spying Amanda's notebook and responding to it as enthusiastically as if it had been a television camera from "Eyewitness News." Amanda didn't even have to open her mouth.

"That dear sweet man," the woman said with heartfelt sincerity. "Why, I declare, I just can't get over it. One minute he's up there saying all those lovely things about chocolate—he has such style, you know—and the next minute he's gone. Whoever will they get to replace him? I just know my family won't have a decent meal without Chef Maurice's recipes to go by."

"So you're a big fan, Mrs. . . . ?"

"Murphy. Elsie Murphy and oh, my, yes, I am a fan. The minute I saw him on his first TV talk show I turned to my husband, I swear I did, and said, 'George, honey, that man is going to be a star.' I made his recipe for coq au vin the very next day. George killed a chicken special, so I could do it."

"I'm sure Chef Maurice would have been pleased to know that," Amanda murmured. "You didn't happen to see anyone suspicious, did you? Maybe somebody who looked as though he was in a hurry?"

"Not that I recall," she said, clearly disappointed that she'd apparently missed out on something. Amanda turned to go. Suddenly brightening, Elsie grabbed her arm. "No, wait. That's not quite true. I saw you run off to the escalator, is that what you mean?"

Amanda winced. "Not exactly, but thanks for your help," she said, hoping that the police didn't question Elsie Murphy too closely now that she'd planted her own behavior in the woman's mind. It would be just her luck to wind up as a suspect. Oscar would love it. It would confirm his suspicions that folks who came out of New York and weren't grateful for the chance to escape were up to no good. The headline would be an inch high:

REPORTER KILLS FOR STORY

She shuddered again and headed back toward the stage, her notebook filled with tributes to Chef Maurice and speculation about what had happened. It was time to find Jonathan Webster again to fill in at least some of the gaps. Before she could locate him, though, a very determined-looking man sauntered up to her, shoved his straw hat back on his head, stared pointedly at her notebook, and demanded, "Okay, honey, just what the hell do you think you're doing?"

Amanda bristled. One delicate blond brow arched significantly as she repeated, "*Honey?* Have we met?"

SHERRY L WOODS

The sarcasm drifted right over his head, which was pretty darn difficult because he appeared to be taller than the average receiver on the Georgia Bulldog football team.

"Joe Donelli," he said in a Brooklyn accent. It tripped Amanda's heartstrings just listening to it. It was the closest she'd come to New York in months, outside of a few quick glimpses of the city during TV reports on the blizzards that had blanketed the East Coast in a foot of snow.

"*Detective* Joe Donelli," he said with added emphasis. "I asked you a question."

Amanda smiled. He didn't need to tell her he was a detective. Detectives and reporters were natural enemies. She could sense the presence of one the way a deer could sniff the scent of a hunter. Besides, normal people did not wear a slightly battered hat pulled low over their eyes in a jaunty manner reminiscent of Mike Hammer. Some people in these parts did wear a baseball cap on the back of their heads while they bounced over the rutted roads in a pickup, but Donelli didn't seem to be in the same league. His hat looked more suitable for a scarecrow. Or maybe a jungle safari.

"I'm Amanda Roberts," she said, steering clear of the question that was uppermost in Detective Donelli's mind. "Interesting case, isn't it? Any idea what caused his death? He was pretty young for a heart attack."

Brown eyes narrowed watchfully. "He was forty-five, not so young to be a prime heart attack candidate, especially if you live on rich sauces and chocolate soufflés."

"So, it was a heart attack then?"

"I didn't say that."

"Then what was it?" She was not about to give him her own ideas on the subject.

"You know, Ms. Roberts, I'm still not sure why you want to know or why you've been badgering the people around here. Don't you think folks are upset enough?"

"Badgering? Who says I've been badgering? I've just been doing my job."

"Which is?"

"I'm a reporter."

Donelli nodded as if she'd just confirmed his worst suspicions.

"I was thinking," she said quickly, flashing him her brightest smile. If it affected him at all, he was a master at disguising his emotions. She decided not to waste any more effort on seductive techniques.

"Maybe we could share information," she suggested. "I mean I was here when it happened and I've interviewed practically everyone. If you could just tell me what you've learned, we could sort of compare notes."

Joe Donelli gave her a slow, lazy smile, a Southern gentleman's smile that was definitely at odds with that Brooklyn accent. Amanda's hopes soared.

"Afraid not," he said, dashing those hopes. "On the other hand, I think it would be mighty nice if you'd just share those notes of yours with me, purely in the interest of helping along the investigation, of course."

As a matter of principle more than anything else, Amanda jammed the notebook into her purse, which was large enough to serve as an overnight bag or a weapon in an emergency. "Not on your life. Come to think of it, I haven't even seen your badge. How do I know you're a detective?"

Joe Donelli looked just the slightest bit embarrassed at that. A lock of his dark hair fell in his face and his brown eyes picked a point in the vicinity of the cheese graters to study with interest. He rocked back on his heels. "I don't exactly have a badge."

"Isn't a detective without a badge sort of like a tree without leaves?"

"You might say I'm sort of an unofficial detective here."

"How unofficial?"

"The man who owns this store is a friend. He's also the sheriff. He knows I used to work homicide in Brooklyn and he asked me to come in as a personal favor and poke around a bit, see if I could come up with anything useful."

"Then you won't mind if I go on with my own unofficial poking around, will you?" Amanda retorted, seizing on the obvious weakness in the man's position to evade his persistent probing. Unfortunately, he seemed to be stubborn, badge or no badge.

"Actually, I do mind that quite a bit. I'd sort of like to see a little spirit of cooperation."

"I'm all for that," Amanda agreed cheerfully. "You first."

"I'd rather start with your notes."

"I'm not feeling quite that civic-minded."

"Then I guess we could discuss them down at the station." He resettled his hat a bit lower over his eyes, but not before Amanda caught what might have been a glint of amusement.

"Are we talking arrest here?"

"Of course not." He looked hurt that she could possibly misconstrue his intentions. Admittedly, it was a nice touch. "Just a little friendly conversation."

"Then, how about a nice cup of coffee right here instead? You can tell me how a cop from Brooklyn ended up in Georgia."

Joe Donelli nodded agreeably, which instantly made Amanda extraordinarily suspicious. "Fine," he said. "Chef Maurice made a fresh pot of coffee right before the demonstration started. I understand he planned to serve it with the soufflé. Want to try some?"

Amanda regarded the podium, where the chef was still lying under that bright red blanket that didn't quite cover his black, wavy hair, the hem of his perfectly creased trousers, or his polished loafers. The thought of drinking his coffee until she knew absolutely for certain why the man was under that blanket didn't appeal to her one bit.

Uttering a sigh of resignation, she gave in. "We'll go to the station."

CHAPTER
Two

AT the tiny one-room police station, which, according to Oscar, had once been a White Castle hamburger place, a single cell had replaced what had apparently been a restroom. A dilapidated cot had been added to the previous equipment. With that stark cell ominously visible, Joe Donelli and Amanda attempted to reach some sort of mutual agreement regarding cooperation. She had the distinct impression, though, that his idea of cooperation was rather one-sided. He was downright obsessed with her notebook.

She could have given it to him without really violating her journalistic obligation to protect her sources. No one had told her anything incriminating as near as she could tell. Still, she felt more secure knowing all those notes were buried under the jelly beans, several pens, her makeup case, and an assortment of crumpled receipts that she always meant to file for her income tax records. It was possible that later on she'd discover some vital piece of evidence had been recorded during those on-the-scene interviews. Then she'd forever regret having handed them over too freely.

Possibly as punishment for her attitude, Donelli left her to sit on a straight-back wooden chair that would have been ideal for torture. While she waited, she idly studied the peeling paint on the wall across from her. Since its White Castle days, the room appeared to have alternated between institutional green and beige. It was now an even less daring shade of gray, as were the two scarred metal desks and the filing cabinet. It was functional enough, but it was even more drab than a Midwestern winter and just as depressing.

As prisons went, this one probably served the purpose well enough. A mere tour of the place ought to keep criminals on the straight and narrow. Chef Maurice's murderer—assuming her cyanide theory was accurate and the chef hadn't done himself in—apparently hadn't paid a visit to the facility or he might have had second thoughts.

Amanda's gaze eventually made its way back to Detective Donelli, who'd been pacing around for the last half hour with the telephone practically glued to his ear. She'd tried eavesdropping on the calls, hoping to pick up some clues about the information that was coming in, but Donelli was a master of mumbled one-word answers.

On the third call he sounded downright expansive and her spirits rose slightly.

"Hey, you're terrific! That's just what we need. How soon can you get over here?"

The possibilities clicked through Amanda's imagination: the coroner's report, a suspect, a credible witness. She forgot all about the peeling paint, the hard chair, and Donelli's reticence. Her fingers practically itched to grab her notebook from the safety of her purse.

Then the perfectly maddening man turned and, without missing a beat, asked quite seriously if she wanted pepperoni on her pizza.

"Pizza?"

"Sure. The sheriff's over in the next town. He said he'd bring one in."

She tried for a measure of dignity when what she wanted to do was jump out of her chair and throttle the man. "I do not want any pizza."

He apparently chose to ignore her haughty tone. "Would you rather have a sandwich? We could be here awhile."

I would rather scream, Amanda thought, but said tersely, "I don't want anything to eat. I want information."

"Sorry. It's not on the menu."

"Then I'll take the damn pizza. No pepperoni, just onions. Lots of onions." Her gray eyes sparked with defiance, though she had a feeling the effect was wasted on Donelli. He beamed at her.

"Hey, great. I love onions."

While Amanda waited impatiently for him to finish, she sorted through her supply of jelly beans until she found some of the pink ones that were flavored like a strawberry daiquiri. She popped several into her mouth. The flavor immediately transported her to a tropical beach, where she wouldn't have to think about a dead chef and an arrogant cop. The tranquillity lasted until Donelli got off the phone.

"Let's try it again," he said, hovering over her in a particularly disturbing way. She wondered if she might be able to make a case for harassment out of it, but doubted it. Looming probably wasn't covered by the law, even if it did make her pulse race against her will.

"What did you see?"

"The same thing you saw: A dead man."

"Nothing suspicious?"

"I thought that was suspicious enough."

Donelli sighed heavily. "Amanda, I thought you were going to cooperate." He sounded very, very disappointed in her. A tiny part of her regretted that, though she wasn't quite sure why.

"That was your idea, not mine," she said anyway. "I'd like to get to the paper and write my story. It would be nice to include the cause of death."

Donelli groaned. "Damn, you're persistent. You'd think this was some big international espionage case or something."

"If you happen to know anything about international espionage, I'll be glad to listen. Meantime, do you know the cause of death or not?"

"Yes. There are still a lot of lab tests to run, but the coroner called earlier with a preliminary ruling."

"Are you going to tell me?"

He shrugged. "I don't see why not. The chef appears to have been poisoned. That little touch of almond flavoring that he said was the secret ingredient in the soufflé turned out to be laced with cyanide. Not very original, when you get right down to it."

"Effective, though," she replied, allowing herself a brief, self-congratulatory cheer.

"Very."

"So what we have here is the murder..."

"Apparent murder."

"What's the alternative? It's certainly a bizarre way to commit suicide."

"It could have been accidental."

She glowered at Donelli. "Okay. *Apparent murder* of an internationally known chef in a town he'd probably never even heard of until the limo dropped him off. How many suspects can there be? It had to be someone who knew the man, unless George Murphy particularly despised having to kill one of his chickens for the chef's coq au vin."

"Who?"

"George Murphy. His wife thought Chef Maurice's recipe for coq au vin was sublime."

"That's the sort of information you have in that notebook of yours?"

"Don't sneer, Donelli. It's more than you have."

"Oh, really," he taunted. He stared at Amanda with dark brown eyes, the sort of soulful eyes that could persuade you of a man's sincerity or get you to reveal your deepest, darkest secrets.

In Amanda's case, he was more interested in the secrets that might have been revealed to her. Now that he'd just discovered that she didn't have any, at least not the sort he'd hoped for, he was very likely to lose interest entirely. Somehow that bothered her more than it should have.

If she could just get out of this crummy police station

so she could go over her notes in peace, she could find the kind of information Donelli was after, the kind that would break this case wide open. She'd laid an entire corruption scandal at the feet of two very proper, highly regarded Manhattan judges, so she could certainly find a murderer in a town that had fewer residents than a big city high school.

"When you leave here, write your story and then stay out of it," Donelli said, as if he'd read her mind. "The police will find out how that cyanide got in Chef Maurice's almond flavoring. We don't need some hotshot reporter messing around and accidentally destroying the evidence or scaring off our killer."

"Killer?"

"Whoever," he corrected quickly. "The sheriff's in charge of the investigation."

"You're not the sheriff. You're not even a deputy," she reminded him.

"In this case, I'm the next best thing."

Amanda didn't want to insult the sheriff's department or its unofficial deputy, but from what she'd seen so far, she thought she had an equal or better shot at beating them to the murderer. Her blood soared through her veins the way it always did when she was after a big story. She assured herself that the sizzling heat that scampered straight to her abdomen could not possibly have anything to do with the way Joe Donelli was looking at her. It might be lust, but it was lust for a major exposé, not for a chauvinistic cop who'd probably been drummed out of Brooklyn because he couldn't handle the tough stuff.

She regarded him curiously. "What are you doing here, Donelli?"

"Checking out a man's death."

"No, I mean what are you doing in a hick town in Georgia looking into a death?" she explained patiently. "What happened back in Brooklyn?"

"Nothing happened. I retired to do some farming."

"Retired?" she repeated. "You're not exactly old enough to be cashing in on your IRA."

"Nope, but being a cop in Brooklyn ages you before your time . . . assuming you live long enough to even get the wrinkles you deserve. After being knifed in the stomach and shot in the back before my thirty-fifth birthday, I decided not to stick around to see if I'd survive 'til forty. Farming seemed like a pleasant alternative."

"Had you ever been on a farm?"

"Nope. I think that's what appealed to me. It would be a whole new *safe* experience. Just about that time, a buddy of mine heard from his second cousin twice removed or some convoluted thing like that. Anyway, the guy had a place down here he wanted to sell. I bought it. It's not exactly Tara in *Gone With the Wind*, but it's all mine."

"How'd your wife feel about all this?"

"My wife stopped feeling anything about my activities sometime between the knifing and the shooting. We're divorced. Works out better all around. She'd hate being so far from Bloomingdale's."

"Isn't Bloomingdale's a little ritzy for a cop's salary?"

"It helped that she had a trust fund," he conceded. "She hardly even noticed when I left."

Amanda found herself torn between compassion and laughter. Because Donelli didn't seem to be feeling one bit sorry for himself, she went with the laughter. "Do you actually know anything about farming?"

He grinned at her. "Not much, but I'm learning. I've mastered tomatoes. Put a little shack on the side of the road and sold 'em all last summer. I felt like a kid with a lemonade stand again. Met a whole bunch of terrific folks who were lost trying to find the right road to Jimmy Carter's place down in Plains. Now I'm thinking of diversifying. I might add onions this year. Maybe even some lettuce."

"Terrific. You'll be able to make a salad and in your spare time, you can play detective."

The remark managed to wipe the smile right off his face. "I don't play at it, Amanda."

As if to prove his point, those brown eyes of his traveled over her with tantalizing slowness. It wasn't a detective's examination of a prime suspect. It was a man's blatant, interested survey of a woman. She immediately felt like checking to make sure all her buttons were still in place.

"You might say I'm a student of human nature," he said with mocking deliberation. "For instance, right now I can tell you're not one bit interested in all this small talk. You're chomping at the bit to get out of here and begin conducting your own investigation. I'd suggest, again, that you keep your pretty little nose out of it until we know what we're up against."

"You can't make me." The remark sounded petulant even to Amanda.

"I wouldn't wager the milk money on that. We could

start by discussing the sentence for withholding evidence," he said and smiled so smugly Amanda wondered what the penalty for assault on a police officer would be. Maybe they could plea bargain.

Fortunately—or unfortunately, depending on your point of view—the sheriff walked in just then with the pizza. His presence dissuaded Amanda from finding out —for the moment. She had a feeling it wouldn't be the last time Joe Donelli would push her to the brink of committing mayhem. He was that sort of man: domineering, arrogant, and sexy as hell.

The sheriff, on the other hand, was tall, thin and as courtly as Clark Gable. Just a shade over fifty, with gray hair at his temples, Bobby Ray Johnson was, in fact, the exact opposite of every movie stereotype of the Southern lawman, until he opened his mouth and spoke with a drawl as thick and sweet as honey.

"Well, boy, what'd you find out over there? They ain't gonna be able to sue that store of mine for negligence, are they?"

Amanda's slice of pizza hovered halfway between the desk and her mouth as she waited for the answer to that one. Donelli looked at the sheriff, looked at her, took a bite of his pizza, and chewed thoughtfully.

"Amanda," he said at last. "I think that'll be all for now. You can run along."

"*Run along?*" she sputtered, eyes glittering. "After sitting here for four solid hours, while you chatted on the phone and hounded me with ridiculous questions, you want me to run along when you're just getting to the good stuff?"

Sheriff Johnson seemed a bit startled by her outburst.

Maybe he'd thought she was Donelli's woman and was just hanging around to keep him company. "Amanda is a reporter," Donelli explained. The sheriff nodded as if that was explanation enough for that infuriating dismissal.

She lifted her chin stubbornly. "I'm not budging. I haven't finished my pizza." She took a bite, a big one, hoping that she wouldn't choke on it.

Donelli rolled his eyes. The sheriff shrugged. And then they began talking as if she weren't even there . . . about fishing. It seemed the sheriff knew a particularly nice spot to catch trout this time of the year, a burbling brook or some damn thing.

"I'll take you up there, boy, just as soon as this case is wrapped up. Amanda, honey, you can come along, too. Biggest fish you ever saw. They practically jump into the boat. We'll build us a campfire and Amanda here can cook 'em right out there in the open. Ain't nothing else like it."

"Sounds like heaven all right," Donelli agreed.

"Sounds like a bunch of bull to me," Amanda mumbled, dropping the rest of her pizza down on the desk, intentionally missing the box. It was a tiny gesture of protest, but it was about as rebellious as she dared to get with that dingy cell staring her in the face.

"I'll walk you to your car," Donelli offered, giving the sheriff a self-satisfied smirk.

"I think I can find my way on my own."

"I'll be in touch, then."

"And I'll be in Scotland before you," she replied pleasantly.

"What is that supposed to mean?" With a movement

so swift it stunned her, he was suddenly marching along right on her heels.

"It's part of an old Scottish ditty. Look it up."

Donelli apparently had no intention of waiting around to check out some lyric. He caught her drift quickly enough. "Don't you dare go out and start poking around on your own, Amanda Roberts. I'll call you when there's something new to report."

"I'll do the same." She was in the car and moving before he could utter the curse that was forming on his lips.

Amanda drove straight through three towns to the little storefront office that was Oscar Cates's excuse for a newsroom. Slightly larger than the police station, it held four desks. In addition to Oscar's and hers, there was one for seventy-six-year-old Wiley Rogers, who turned up his hearing aid and took the classifieds over the phone one day a week. There was also a spare for that glorious day when there would actually be a full-time sports reporter, instead of a high school kid who came in for two hours on Tuesdays after school to write a wrap-up of the previous week's games. Amanda's desk had a rose on it in defiance of Oscar's attempt to make the place resemble a pigsty. In addition to the surface clutter, there were several file cabinets with their drawers bulging with material in no particular order since 1957, when the file clerk had left to have a baby.

"Where the dickens have you been?" Oscar groused the minute she walked in the door. "Larry's done been here and gone. Left me quite a spread. Want to take a look?"

Pictures were strewn across his desktop. For a man with Oscar's tabloid instincts, it was heady stuff. There was Chef Maurice with his face buried in chocolate. There was Chef Maurice under the blanket with Jonathan Webster and Sarah Robbins sobbing in each other's arms as stunned onlookers milled around. There was even one of an adoring fan trying to tuck an artificial flower she'd obviously plucked from her hat under the edge of the blanket. A poster of a beaming Chef Maurice hovered obscenely in the background of each and every shot.

"Great, ain't it?"

"It sure beats the annual pie-eating contest," Amanda said as a shiver of disgust ran along her spine. She went to her desk and began shuffling the stacks of handwritten notices sent in by the paper's scattered correspondents. "Have you seen my file?"

"Which file is that?"

"The one I put together on Chef Maurice. I thought there might be something in it that would help."

"Help what? Ain't Bobby Ray got this whole thing under wraps by now?"

"He didn't when I left the jail twenty minutes ago." She shot a determined glance at her boss, who'd been trying to take a discreet swig of bourbon while her back was turned. "I'm going to break this story wide open, Oscar. I'm going to find the murderer."

Oscar did not look respectful. He looked worried. "I don't think it's such a good idea for you to go messing around in this, Amanda. Don't you think maybe you ought to leave it to the professionals?"

"I am a professional."

"I meant a professional law enforcement officer."

"Bobby Ray is hardly that. He won the last election because no one else in the county felt like running. You told me that yourself." She regarded him thoughtfully. "You aren't scared of the man, are you? Are you worried he'll pull his store ads or something?"

"Of course not." Oscar's face was red with indignation. "I'm just worrying about you, little lady. I mean that chef is flat-out dead and all. No telling why he got that way. Maybe there's a homicidal maniac on the loose." Amanda wasn't absolutely certain, but Oscar appeared to be licking his lips at that particular prospect.

"Then somebody had best be finding the maniac before the whole town ends up dead," she said, lapsing into her increasingly frequent tendency to mimic Oscar's drawl. "That somebody is going to be me. Now where's the file?"

Oscar gave a little sigh of resignation. "Right here. I was looking through it."

"See anything interesting?" She sat on a corner of her desk, just because she knew it drove Oscar crazy. He scowled at her, but he was apparently too interested in the murder to waste time on a lecture about newsroom decorum.

"Not a durn thing," he said. "Just a bunch of highfalutin nonsense about what a genius Chef Maurice is. The usual PR stuff."

"No background? Marriages? Nasty divorces?"

"Nope. It's like the guy came to earth fully grown with no attachments."

Amanda lifted the lid on the jar of jelly beans on her desk and took out one of the ice blue mint kind. She popped it in her mouth and sucked on it thoughtfully. "Do you think that could be significant?"

"Personally, I think it's downright peculiar. Everybody's got a past. What about that PR guy who was with him? Larry said the guy was slicker than an oil spill."

"Oscar, you're a genius," Amanda said, surprising him by jumping up to bestow a kiss on his balding head. "I'd been meaning to get back to Jonathan Webster when Donelli dragged me down to the sheriff's office."

"Who the devil's Donelli?"

"You don't want to know. Just get on the phone and help me call the hotels in Atlanta and see if we can track down Webster. I doubt if he's staying out at some motel on the highway. He's probably at one of those posh places in downtown with room service and a phone in the bathroom."

They found him on the fourth try. He was registered at the Hyatt, the same place that had held its annual chocolate lover's festival the previous weekend. Her pulse racing, Amanda was out the door before the bemused Oscar had time to blink, much less hoist his bulk out of his chair to come after her. She heard him warning her to be careful as she roared down Main Street.

CHAPTER
Three

JONATHAN Webster was drunk. The beige jacket had been tossed carelessly on the floor of his hotel suite. He had one shoe on; the other, unaccountably, was sitting on an end table like some sort of avant-garde ashtray. A bottle of vodka, three-fourths empty, was tucked under his arm when he opened the door. His glazed-over eyes tried to focus and failed. He simply turned around, weaved his way back into the pitch dark room, and collapsed on the sofa, leaving it to Amanda to follow or not.

She followed, stopping long enough to flip on the lights, then pick up the phone and call room service for two pots of very black, very strong coffee. She was particularly emphatic about it being strong. Jonathan Webster eyed her warily as she plunked the phone receiver back into place.

"I won't drink it, you know," he said with surprising force and clarity.

"Then I will. It's been a long day."

He stared at her, as if trying to puzzle something out. "We met at the store, didn't we? You're that reporter—Rogers, Roberts, something like that."

"You must not be as drunk as I thought. It's Roberts. Amanda Roberts."

"Oh, I am very drunk," Jonathan Webster corrected, "but not nearly as drunk as I'd like to be or plan to be and not nearly drunk enough to forget one single minute of this afternoon's godawful events. I suppose that's what you're here about."

Amanda nodded. "I want to know about Chef Maurice. Anything you can tell me: where he was from; how he got started; his family; how he behaved when he wasn't onstage. I want the works."

"Didn't you get our press kit?"

"I did and it was lovely. Very classy, in fact. Including a few new recipes was a nice touch. I'm not sure you'll find any takers for the chocolate soufflé after what happened, though."

Jonathan Webster buried his face in his hands and groaned. "Don't remind me. I thought traveling around the country with a superstar cat was as low as I would ever go, but this . . . this has been the darkest day of my less than illustrious career."

"It wasn't exactly a red-letter day for Chef Maurice, either. Would you care to speculate on what went wrong?"

"If you want speculation, go to the police. If you want information about the chef, read your press kit. I'm busy getting drunk." To emphasize his point, he tilted the bottle up and swallowed greedily.

Amanda decided to ignore the defiant gesture. "Actually your press kit was surprisingly devoid of personal details. I thought you might know more."

"If you read it, you know as much as I do. When I went to work for Chef Maurice, that was the material I was given. Someone—don't ask me who—decided it would be best to keep an aura of mystery about him."

"Any idea why?"

"Maybe the man had a police record. I don't know. I always thought it was a particularly risky tactic. That kind of thing practically invites some curious reporter to go poking around looking for dirt. But the guy was adamant and when you're as successful as he is, nobody argues with you."

"Someone did," Amanda pointed out.

Jonathan Webster smiled at that, a weary sort of salute to a mild joke. "Ah, but that's where you're wrong. There were no shouts, no threats. Nobody waved a gun or even stabbed him in the back. Someone just quietly laced his cooking ingredients with a little dollop of cyanide. I personally thought it made up in subtlety what it lacked in originality. Unlike many of my peers, who like to do things with a flourish, I have a particular appreciation for subtlety."

The arrival of the coffee and Joe Donelli at the same time prevented any need for Amanda to respond to that. She would have found a straight-faced reply particularly difficult because Jonathan Webster was still wearing his pink T-shirt. He was also sitting in a hotel suite that probably cost well over $100 a night and drinking an extraordinarily expensive brand of vodka straight from the bottle he brandished about as he talked. She considered the appearance of the coffee particularly timely. She was less thrilled about Donelli.

"Having a party?" Donelli asked.

"A wake," Jonathan Webster replied. "Join us and share your memories of the late chef."

"Since he was dead when we met, I doubt I'd have much to contribute to the conversation. I think I'll just listen." He settled back in a chair, slid his hat to the back of his head, and looked at the two of them with interest. "Well?"

"Oh, what the hell," Amanda mumbled, scowling at Donelli. "I was just about to ask Mr. Webster if Chef Maurice had any enemies."

"Good question," Donelli said approvingly. "Slightly predictable, but all the same it needs answering."

Amanda began to grind her teeth. If this kept up, she was going to be back at the dentist being treated for an out of line jaw. It would be one thing to develop the latest Yuppie stress disorder under deadline pressures in Washington; it was quite another to contemplate developing it here. She drew in a calming breath as she waited for Jonathan Webster's reply to her good, predictable question.

"If he had any enemies, he hid them from me."

"Family, then?"

"None listed in my files."

"Anyone in the crowd who looked familiar? Some groupie who's been in other cities perhaps?"

There was a slight hesitation, a faint flicker of something in his eyes, then a shake of his head. "No."

"Are you sure?" Donelli asked, pouncing on the hesitation with admirable alertness. "You looked as though there might have been someone."

"There was one man I had the feeling I'd seen somewhere before. Something about his eyes, but it was very vague. I can't be sure."

"Think, man. It could be important."

"I told you it was only an impression."

"What about friends?" Amanda asked. "Did he have any special friends?"

Jonathan Webster allowed himself a discreet smile. "He was a very good-looking man."

"You're saying there were women," Donelli interpreted unnecessarily.

Discretion flew out the window and the smile widened. "Flocks of them."

"Any one woman who was around more than the rest?"

"He'd been in sixty cities in the last three months. That hardly allows enough time to strike up an enduring relationship."

"Before that?" Donelli persisted.

"As I told Ms. Roberts, as far as I'm concerned, Chef Maurice had no life before that. I came on board for the tour. I was hired by a New York agency, given an itinerary, a bundle of press kits, and a list of contacts. He didn't offer me his diary."

"Any controversy on the tour?" Donelli asked. "Maybe some newspaper food writer who didn't like his recipes? A fan he ignored?"

"Nothing."

"Did he bring his own supplies with him to each

city?" Amanda asked, earning a grudging look of admiration from Donelli.

"Some of them. For the most part, though, we sent a list on ahead and the stores supplied them."

"Did anyone check them before the demonstration?"

"I did, just to make sure everything was there."

"What time?"

"About eleven-thirty, as soon as we arrived from Atlanta."

"And the demonstration began on time?"

"Promptly at noon. It was one of the chef's hang-ups. He refused to keep people waiting."

"Think carefully. Was the almond extract there when you checked?" Donelli moved to the edge of his chair.

"Absolutely. There was nothing missing or I would have made a note of it."

"Was it an unopened bottle?"

"It was still in the box. I didn't open the bottle to see if the seal had been broken. I had no reason to."

"Who, besides you, had access to the ingredients during that half hour?"

"You'd have to check with store security or that Robbins woman about that. I doubt if they were kept in the safe, if that's what you mean. Most thieves these days are after more than eggs and baking chocolate," Webster said with what Amanda considered to be an unnecessary touch of sarcasm.

"That doesn't exactly help to narrow down the list of suspects, does it?" she said in disappointment.

Donelli grinned. "Not much, but it was a nice try. At least we have a pretty good idea when the tampering took place."

"I can live without any pats on the head from you."

"Be thankful that's all I'm doing," he murmured. Only Amanda was attuned to the dire overtone of the comment. It was the first overt sign of Donelli's displeasure since he'd walked in and found her one step ahead of him. "Why don't we get out of here, Amanda, and let Mr. Webster get some rest?"

Amanda was out of questions for the moment, but she wasn't ready to be herded out the door by a man who was very likely to give her another lecture. "I'm not quite through," she replied.

Donelli leaned against the door frame and waited. Humphrey Bogart couldn't have made the stance any more masculine.

"You can go on, if you want," she encouraged.

"That's okay. I don't mind waiting."

"Never mind," she grumbled, getting to her feet. "I'll talk to Mr. Webster later when there are fewer interruptions."

There was an exchange of pleasantries at the door and then Donelli's hand was on her elbow. Trepidation was setting off little flares of warning in her stomach and Jonathan Webster was quietly closing the door on the only escape she had from Donelli's expected display of temper.

"Aren't you going to warn him not to leave town?" she asked, hoping to distract him.

"We discussed the need for his continued presence earlier in the day. He seems like a smart man. I doubt he'll forget it." He scowled down at her. "You, on the other hand, don't seem to listen to a damn thing I say."

"I'm not a suspect," she offered with what she thought was great originality of thought.

"No," Donelli said agreeably, as he guided her into the elevator. "But, as you have just surmised, Jonathan Webster is. Did it occur to you that he might have a stake in shutting you up? Dammit, Amanda, use your head."

The hairs on the back of Amanda's neck stood straight up, but she said bravely, "Don't you think you're being a little melodramatic? If Jonathan Webster killed Chef Maurice, he must have had a reason. He doesn't have any reason to kill me."

"Unless he happens to decide you're getting too close to the truth."

"But I don't know anything," she protested, ignoring Donelli's groan of disgust.

"Yet," she amended, just in case he was about to make some assumptions about her professional skills.

"Amanda, this is not a game."

Amanda was tired and frustrated. The threads of her story were all tangled up and it was likely to be days before she could untangle them. And she was sick to death of being treated as though her intelligence were only one step higher than that of a jackrabbit.

"I am not treating it like a game," she snapped with indignation, handing her parking voucher over to the doorman. "I know the risks here, just as well as you do."

"Do you really?"

"All right, Donelli, since you seem to think I'm a menace to myself and the investigation, let's trade credentials. I know yours. Now let's talk about mine. Are you at all familiar with the Yankovich bribery scandal in New York or were you too busy handing out parking tickets to notice?"

He ignored the jibe and asked, "You mean that case that tumbled two judges straight into the slammer?"

"That's the one."

"What about it?"

"It was my story."

"Yours?" His disbelieving reaction would not have provided much sustenance for a starving ego.

"Mine. Every Pulitzer Prize-contending word of it."

"It was a hell of a story," he conceded. "It wasn't a murder, though."

"I received death threats on the average of once a week the entire time I was investigating the story. When it broke, the threats got a little more frequent, to say nothing of more serious. Several were accompanied by bullets whizzing through the living room window of my apartment. One was emphasized by a rather dramatic car bomb. I spent the last two weeks I worked on that story hidden away in some fleabag hotel with rotating vice cops as companions. Not even my husband knew where I was. To sum it up, I am not as naive or as careless as you seem to think."

"Okay. I stand corrected. You're not naive. Maybe you've just developed some sort of death wish. That doesn't mean I have to go along with it. I still don't like the idea of your putting your neck on the line one bit better."

"The women on the Brooklyn police force must have loved you."

Donelli swallowed hard.

"Hit a sore spot, did I?" she said cheerfully.

"How I felt about female police officers is hardly the point. At least they had guns and they knew how to use them."

"What makes you think I don't?"

"Do you?"

"No."

"I rest my case."

He tucked her into her car as protectively as any mother ever tucked blankets around her baby, then leaned in the window. "By the way, what was that bit about a husband?"

Amanda was thrown by the non sequitur. Despite her irritation, she smiled. "An ex-husband now."

He nodded in satisfaction and Amanda felt a stirring of entirely unexpected and unwanted anticipation.

"Don't take any side trips on the way home," he warned. "I'll be right behind you."

"Are you coming in for coffee?" The words were out of her mouth before she could stop them. She wasn't sure who was more astonished.

Even an obtuse man could have heard the unexpected hint of wistfulness in her voice and Donelli, for all of his flaws, wasn't one bit obtuse. He grinned. "No," he said. "But thanks for asking."

"Oh," she said flatly.

"Another time."

Suddenly furious with herself for allowing him to see even the tiniest hint of vulnerability, she snapped, "Don't count on it."

Donelli was still standing in the road when she took off, though he caught up with her minutes later on the highway and stayed a respectable two car-lengths behind all the way home. He blinked his lights when she turned into her driveway. The gesture was equal parts comforting and exasperating.

In the end, though, it turned out to be a darn good thing that Joe Donelli had more restraint than she did. She would have hated like hell for him to have been one step behind her when she walked up to her front porch and found Sarah Robbins sitting right there in one of the wicker rocking chairs.

Hiding her astonishment, Amanda crossed the porch and sat down next to her.

"I hope you don't mind my coming over here," Sarah said. "I checked the phone book and found out where you lived."

"I don't mind," Amanda said, noting that the woman was still dressed in the same skirt and blouse, which were considerably the worse for wear. Sarah's dark hair was mussed, and even in the dim light Amanda could see that her hands trembled.

"It's just that you were so sympathetic this morning and I don't have many friends down here yet and, well, I just couldn't face going back to an empty apartment after what happened."

"I see." Amanda had long ago learned that sometimes the best interviewing technique was to just keep your mouth shut.

"I've read your stories," Sarah said suddenly. "Not that they give you much to do on that paper. All those little social items about Mrs. So-and-so's grandson being here for a visit and Mr. High-and-mighty's mother going to the Mayo Clinic for a checkup. It must drive you crazy, but you have a nice touch. You can tell you're a sympathetic sort of person."

"Thank you."

"Do you believe in fate, Ms. Roberts?"

Actually, philosophically speaking, Amanda believed one controlled one's own destiny, but she supposed there was room for doubt. If it would get Sarah Robbins to open up, she'd have declared a belief in the tooth fairy. Just for argument's sake, of course.

"To a certain extent," she equivocated.

"I do. I believe that our lives take off on a certain course and no matter what we do to try to stop things, it's beyond our control. I would have stopped Chef Maurice from dying, if I could have." She peered at Amanda intently. "But don't you see, once he'd agreed to come here, it was out of my hands."

"In what way? Do you know something about this, Ms. Robbins, something you haven't told the sheriff or Detective Donelli? Did you see someone tampering with the chef's ingredients?"

"No, but I do know that not everyone loved him as I did. I thought he was a genius," she confided. "There are others, though, who were jealous of his success. Any one of them might have decided to stop him."

"Who, Sarah? Who was jealous of him? Is that something you read?"

"No, I just knew it."

"How? I don't understand."

"Isn't that what always happens when someone rises above the rest?"

"So this is just a theory? You don't have anyone specific in mind?"

Sarah started to say more, then sighed heavily. "So many questions," she said with an elusive smile. "For a moment there, I almost forgot you were a reporter, my dear. I've probably said too much already."

Amanda was torn. If she encouraged Sarah to go on, if she let her confide her story off the record, she would regret it later. And yet she sensed the woman's desperate need to talk.

"I'm sorry to have troubled you," Sarah said.

The weary, lonely tone of the words frightened Amanda. For once, it seemed, there was something more important than the story.

"You haven't troubled me. Please, stay longer, if you don't feel like going home alone. I have a guest room. You can spend the night."

"That's very kind of you, but no. Perhaps the drive will be good for me. I like to think while I drive and tonight I have quite a lot of thinking to do."

"Give me your phone number then, so I can call you," Amanda said, feeling an urgency she couldn't explain.

"There's no need."

"I know that. I'd like to stay in touch."

An eerie sort of smile again played about Sarah's lips. "I think we could have been friends, if we'd had the chance," she said.

"We still can be."

Sarah squeezed her hand then and without another word vanished into the shadows. It was only after her car had started and she'd driven down the lane that

Amanda realized that the woman hadn't left her phone number.

Often during the next few days, Amanda thought about Sarah Robbins and wondered how much she really knew. She'd had the distinct feeling that Sarah was holding something very specific back, that she'd been on the verge of confessing something important. Once Amanda even called her at the store to follow up on her hunch. She was told that Sarah had taken a few days off. The clerk took Amanda's number and offered a vague promise to pass on the message. Amanda vowed to call again, then put the poor, distraught woman out of her mind and spent the next week on the phone following up other leads, pointedly ignoring Joe Donelli's advice to stay out of the case.

Her investigation turned up some interesting information about Jonathan Webster. His reputation in public relations had been on a downhill slide until he'd landed the Chef Maurice tour several months earlier. Just as Sarah Robbins had surmised, the two had become friends, but lately there had been some public arguments. There were rumors in New York that Chef Maurice had been looking for a new public relations representative to complete the tour.

Was that sufficient motive for murder? More than likely, Amanda thought. Certainly Jonathan Webster had had access to Chef Maurice's supplies. He'd admitted that and the store staff would have thought nothing of allowing him to check out the ingredients before the demonstration. He could have doctored the almond flavoring. Ironically, though it was an easy explanation, she didn't think that he had done it. She'd been there at the instant he discovered that Chef Maurice was dead. She'd seen the look of genuine astonishment in his eyes. She'd also seen the momentary panic. Now that panic could have resulted from the fear of being discovered. More likely, now that she knew about his situation, it had been panic about the future.

So, if Jonathan Webster hadn't done it, who had? She sat at her kitchen table on Sunday morning with her notes spread out and a cup of coffee in her hand. When Joe Donelli knocked on the screen door, she was just thinking of drawing a diagram of the scene to nudge her memory into recalling exactly where everyone had been standing. At the sight of Donelli, she forgot about her diagram and tried to figure out how she could hide her notes when they were already in plain view.

"I hear you're still asking questions," Donelli said, opening the door and heading straight for the coffeepot without waiting for her to tell him to come in. The man was definitely pushy. A southern gentleman would stay the hell out of her kitchen until he'd been invited in. Donelli apparently wasn't taking any chances that such an invitation might not be forthcoming.

"What are you doing here?"

"I came for that coffee you offered."

"That was last week."

"Isn't the offer still good?"

"Does it matter? You already have a cup and it's clear you're not about to leave."

"You're very perceptive."

"Not really. I still don't know why you're really here."

"I came to do you a favor."

"Really?" Her tone and the expression in her gray eyes were decidedly skeptical.

"I came to warn you one last time to let the police handle this investigation. Despite what you told me the other night, I'm more convinced than ever that you're in over your head, Amanda. Bobby Ray's worried about you, too. He asked me to try again to talk some sense into you."

"What on earth's wrong with the two of you? It's a simple little murder, probably a one-shot deal, according to all your official police statements. A crime of passion, you might say."

"An apt description," Donelli said agreeably. "It more or less explains why one of the witnesses turned up dead this morning in Atlanta."

Amanda swallowed the lump that suddenly formed in her throat. Then her eyes lit up and she grabbed her pen and a notebook. "Which one?"

"Sarah Robbins."

An image of Sarah Robbins sobbing into her handkerchief popped into Amanda's mind. The image that lingered, though, was of Sarah Robbins sitting on the front porch on a moonlit night with the scent of roses in the air talking about fate. A chill of apprehension swept over her.

"Who'd want to kill her? She was just an innocuous little nobody. That doesn't make any sense."

"It does when you read the note Bobby Ray found beside her body when he went over there to question her this morning. It seems Ms. Robbins, formerly Sandra Reynolds, was once involved with the good chef. It's not entirely clear yet exactly how they met or how long ago it all happened. Anyway, she said she'd taken the job at Bobby Ray's store a few weeks ago and encouraged the store to book Chef Maurice for this demonstration."

Huge chunks of Sarah Robbins's disjointed conversation began to make sense. "I want to see the note. I want to see exactly what she said."

"The Atlanta police have the original. I left a copy of it down at the station for Bobby Ray. I suppose it wouldn't hurt for you to drop by tomorrow to see it. Is there something in particular you're looking for?"

"No. It's just a feeling I have that there might be more there that you're not seeing. She told me she felt responsible for bringing him here. I assumed she thought it would be good for business."

"I don't think so. Sounded to me like she was simply hoping that seeing him again would rekindle the old romance. Apparently it didn't work."

"Are you suggesting she reacted in a rage to being the scorned lover, killed him, and then committed suicide?"

"That's one interpretation. The Atlanta police like it."

"I don't buy it. I talked to her. In fact, she was here the other night."

"She was here?"

"She needed somebody to talk to."

"Tell me about it."

Amanda repeated the gist of the conversation. "She seemed like a quiet, unassuming woman. Sad, actually.

More the type to pine away in silence than to publicly kill an ex-lover and then do away with herself."

Donelli sighed. "Frankly, that's what I thought, too, which is why I'm warning you again to stay away from this. There are two people dead already. Let's not go for three."

"I'll be careful. Thanks for dropping by with the news. I'll stop by the station tomorrow for a look at that suicide note."

"That sounds like a dismissal. Are you in a hurry?"

Amanda flushed guiltily. "No. Of course not. Finish your coffee."

"You don't sound sincere. I assume that means you have your own theories you can't wait to check out."

She saw no point in lying to the man's face. "I'm beginning to," she admitted.

"I should have known. Let's go to brunch and you can tell me all about them."

"Why don't we wait until I see if anything comes of my ideas?"

Donelli just stared at her and waited.

"Oh, all right. I'll fill you in. On one condition," Amanda grumbled, stuffing her notes and a new supply of jelly beans into her purse.

"What's that?"

"We have brunch in Atlanta."

"Why Atlanta? There's a great place out on the highway." He grimaced. "Never mind. I don't think I want to hear the answer to that."

"I'll tell you anyway. We're having brunch in Atlanta because we're not going to eat until right after we visit the scene of Sarah Robbins's death."

Donelli shook his head. "Forget it."

"Okay. I'll go alone."

He studied her curiously. "Aren't you afraid of losing your appetite?"

"I have a strong stomach, Donelli. What about you?"

He glowered as he stalked to the door and held it open. "Come on, Amanda."

She stood facing him, her chin tilted at a stubborn angle. "Where are we going?"

He hesitated, then sighed. "To the station to see that note and then to Atlanta."

"Thanks, Donelli."

"Don't mention it." His expression was fierce, but Amanda saw just the tiniest glimmer of respect in his dark eyes. It made her feel astonishingly good inside.

"One other thing," he said.

"Yes?"

"Try not to leave any fingerprints behind."

CHAPTER
Four

MEN and their cars, Amanda thought with tolerant amusement as she regarded Donelli's aging, scarred Chevy up close for the first time. The red paint was faded and chipped, the much dented bumpers were clearly a victim of the Brooklyn traffic wars, the upholstery had been worn thin, and the engine coughed and sputtered belligerently when he tried the key in the ignition. But once it started, surprisingly it purred with an almost silent hum.

After waiting patiently for her to buckle her seat belt, Donelli drove the decrepit car as if he were protecting a $35,000 investment in a sleek new Mercedes. He grimaced each time the car bounced over an unavoidable pothole. The speedometer never once crept over a sedate forty-nine, probably because it couldn't, she thought disparagingly. Or maybe Donelli was just one of those rarities—a cop who didn't violate the traffic laws.

As if his slow speed weren't irritating enough, the

radio was tuned to a country music station where the grating twang of guitars and whiskey-roughened voices set a mood that was edged with melancholy. By the time George Strait began singing "All My Ex's Live in Texas," Amanda was ready to get out and walk to Atlanta.

"I think you've acclimated too well, Donelli."

He glanced at her curiously.

"The music."

"At least this stuff makes sense. That song was up for a Grammy last year. I listened to country music long before I moved down here. If you want lyrics that are filled with honest emotion, instead of some screaming gibberish, you can't beat it."

Amanda rolled her eyes, sank farther down in the seat, and tried to block out the honest emotion of Johnny Cash, Hank Williams Jr., Dolly Parton, some group called The Judds, and Willie Nelson. When the DJ announced Reba McIntire's hit, "The Last One to Know," however, she found her thoughts drifting unexpectedly and traitorously back to Mack Roberts and the last days of their marriage. Suddenly, there was a lump in her throat and she realized that no matter how fully recovered you thought you were after a divorce, no matter how right you knew the decision had been, it was always possible to resurrect the pain. She glared at Donelli as if it were his fault that she was suddenly feeling lousy.

In an attempt to focus on something other than the haunting lyrics, she concentrated on how miserably uncomfortable she was. The July heat rose up from the pavement in shimmering waves. The still air was so humid that it plastered her blouse to her back. As a

distraction it worked very well. Combined with everything else, it was enough to set her teeth on edge all
over again. Why had she agreed to make this trip with
Donelli? She had always worked alone. This was no
time to be changing that successful pattern.

Fortunately, before she could sink even further into
depression, they reached the sheriff's office. Donelli ran
in and came back out with the copy of the suicide note.
He handed it to her with no comment.

She opened the folded page and with a sense of in-
vading the other woman's privacy, she studied it closely.
"What kind of paper was this written on?" she asked at
once.

"Plain white typing paper. Pretty ordinary. Why?"

"And the ink?"

"Amanda! What are you getting at?"

"Just answer me."

"It looked like a ballpoint pen."

"Hmm."

"Hmm what, dammit?"

"Sarah struck me as the type of woman who'd have
expensive stationery and use a fountain pen. Everything
about her was classy."

"So you think . . ."

"That someone else chose this for her."

While Donelli pondered that possibility, she began to
read. Sadly, she noted that the note was addressed to no
one in particular.

*I'm sorry. I didn't mean for it to end this way. No
matter how it looks, I loved Maurice. That's why I
took the job, why I arranged the demonstration. I*

only wanted to see him again. I never meant for things to get out of hand. I never meant for him to die. I should have known it couldn't work. I should have realized. It's my fault and I can't live with that. Perhaps God will be kind and I will be with Maurice when this is over. Sandra Reynolds (Sarah Robbins)

So, there it was, an admission of complicity in Chef Maurice's death. But was it an admission of murder? It didn't sound like it to Amanda. She was more convinced than ever that Sarah Robbins or Sandra Reynolds or whatever she wanted to call herself had simply been a pitiful, lonely woman who'd wanted nothing more than another chance with her ex-lover. It saddened Amanda that that simple desire had ended so tragically for two people. She wondered once more, though, if Sarah had known more than she'd revealed in the note. It seemed she'd had some sort of premonition that this trip could endanger the chef. Had she guessed the identity of the killer? For that matter had she been forced to write this vague admission before being killed herself?

As they finally approached Sarah's apartment in the trendy Virginia-Highland area of Atlanta, Amanda's mood deteriorated even further. Taking it out on Donelli, she grumbled, "How do you stand riding around in this heat? Haven't you ever heard of air-conditioning?"

"Didn't need it in Brooklyn."

"You're not in Brooklyn now." A belligerent trickle of sweat ran into her eye and she blinked hard at the salty sting. Without comment, Donelli reached in the back pocket of his faded jeans and handed her a plaid hand-kerchief.

It was obvious they both knew her renewed bad temper had very little to do with the car's lack of air-conditioning.

"You don't like it here much, do you?" he asked, studying her quizzically.

"Not much."

"Why not? It's a great place, if you give it a chance."

"It's not New York."

"No, thank goodness." When she didn't respond to his heartfelt sentiment, he said, "You could always leave. A reporter with your track record should be able to land a job on any paper in the country. Or are you more reluctant to walk away from that ex-husband of yours than you've admitted?"

Amanda rubbed viciously at the trail of sweat and snapped, "Don't be ridiculous. Besides, what makes you think my ex-husband is here?"

"It's the only thing that makes sense. The way you carry on about New York, you would never have moved here on your own. I figure he came down here to teach, fell for some kid at the university, and you split."

Amanda's eyes widened, then narrowed suspiciously.

"Am I right?" he asked.

"How did you know that?"

"I'm a good cop, Amanda. When will you get that through your head?"

"You checked on me?"

"I didn't exactly run an FBI printout on you, so get that indignant frown off your face. I just asked around here and there."

"Why?"

"Maybe I just liked your looks."

"You what! Of all the . . ."

"Would you rather I had said I considered you a suspect?"

"At least it would have been more professional."

"It would also have sullied your sterling reputation. Were you prepared for that?"

"I don't much care what the people around here think of me."

"Then you won't want to hear what I heard at the 7-11, will you?" he teased. At least she thought he was teasing.

"Go to hell, Donelli."

He chuckled. "Okay, seriously, Amanda. Where do you want to go after you leave Georgia?"

"Anyplace."

"There are papers in Mississippi."

She scowled. "Okay. Forget anyplace. I want to go North. I want to head an investigative unit on one of the major papers—*The New York Times, The Washington Post*. I want to be someplace where what I write will be read by people who can make changes."

Donelli whistled, though she had a feeling he wasn't particularly impressed by her goal. "No more small-time stuff."

"Exactly."

"Is this story your ticket out of here?"

"Hardly. The Yankovich story will get me out of here eventually. I just have to wait for the right opening. In the meantime, this story is the key to my sanity."

"Running low on challenges, are you?" he said with a

depth of understanding and sympathy that surprised her. Amanda met his sudden grin and smiled back ruefully.

"Yep. Once I conquered mildew, it started going downhill from there. What about you? After a lifetime in Brooklyn, this can't have been a particularly easy transition for you either."

"You're wrong. I was more than ready to give up living on the edge. It's a good feeling to look at the sunset and see the colors, instead of wondering how long it'll be before the liquor store is held up or when the first little old lady will be mugged on her way home from evening mass."

"I see your point, but you were making a contribution then. Now you're just existing."

"Contribution, hell. I was just cleaning up after the crimes, not preventing them. For every creep I put away, two more moved in to take his place."

"But you can't stop trying."

"That's where you're wrong. I walked away and there's no turning back."

"If you were able to put it behind you so easily, why are you involved in this case?"

"I told you. I'm doing it for a friend."

"And if Bobby Ray hadn't asked, you'd be perfectly content to yank the weeds out of your garden all day?" she said. "I don't believe it. Don't forget, I saw you in that store, poking around, asking questions. There was no mistaking the excitement. You love this stuff just as much as I do, Donelli. You like finding all the little pieces and putting them together. You'd never be content to spend the rest of your life just playing Clue on

Saturday nights with the neighbors. You crave the real thing."

He didn't deny it, but he was very quick to try to change the subject. "How'd we get started talking about me? You're the one who's playing amateur detective. Give it up, Amanda."

"And let you have all the fun? I don't think so. I like puzzles, too."

"Maybe we could make a pact."

She eyed him suspiciously. "What sort of pact?"

"I'll keep you informed of everything that's happening. I'll even bounce my ideas about the case off you. You'll have all the pieces of the puzzle that I have."

"But?"

His steady gaze left the road and met hers, his eyes filled with innocence. "But what?"

"There has to be a hitch. You're not the sort of cop to team up with someone you consider to be a rogue reporter. What do you want from from me in return?"

"You're not going to like it."

"Probably not. Tell me anyway."

"I want the same thing I've wanted all along. I want you to sit on that front porch of yours and sip lemonade. If you insist on working, stick to covering garden parties. In other words, I want you to stop poking around in something that could get you killed."

"No way."

"Don't argue with me, Amanda. I have a bad feeling about this case. Couldn't you just for once listen to someone who cares about your welfare?"

"Who are you trying to kid? You don't give a flying fig about my welfare, Donelli. I'm not some frail

Southern flower who's likely to wilt at the first sign of danger. You're only interested in your own ego, which will be severely bruised if I break this case before you do."

"Oh, for . . ."

She didn't wait for the angry tirade she was sure was coming. "And what about you? Couldn't this good deed of yours get you killed, too? Or do you wear a bullet-proof vest at all times?"

"I don't think guns are our killer's style."

Amanda glared at him. "You're a real wiseass, Donelli. Let me rephrase the question: Do you plan to have all your meals tested for poison?"

"If you're asking if I think I'm immune to the killer's wrath, the answer is no. But I'm not just being a macho jerk, either. I'm in a much better position to protect myself than you are."

"So, we're back to the gun bit again," she said in disgust.

"Not exactly. We're back to the fact that I'm a veteran police officer with training in marksmanship and karate."

"That's why you got yourself shot and knifed, I suppose."

Donelli's hands tightened on the steering wheel and Amanda felt an instant pang of regret for the sarcastic comment. The car spun around a corner on two wheels and screeched to a halt in front of a small apartment complex with white shutters and wrought-iron railings. The momentary burst of recklessness told her more than anything else exactly how infuriated he was. He switched off the ignition with slow deliberation and then turned to face her. Tiny white lines at the corners of his mouth emphasized his tension. There were anger and pain in the depths of those brown eyes. Despite herself Amanda felt his hurt.

"I got knifed by a punk kid, no more than thirteen years old, who was high on drugs. I was trying to pull him off my partner—my female partner, one of the best cops I ever knew—when the knife caught me in the chest and slashed all the way up to my throat," he said matter-of-factly. "Fortunately, it wasn't much more than a surface wound or we wouldn't be having this conversation."

Amanda blinked and swallowed hard.

"As for the bullet, I took it in the back, less than one inch from my spinal cord. Someone wasn't happy with my investigation into the ties between the mob and some of the teen street gangs in the city. They pulled the gun on me as I was walking into a McDonald's to get a cup of coffee. That's two incidents, Amanda. That's just twice out of those thousands of calls I answered during nearly fifteen years on the force. That's a damn sight more than luck and a hell of a better record than you have."

"I'm sorry," she said, suddenly feeling lousy and fighting an urge to cry. "I really am. I'm sorry it happened to you and I'm sorry I made such an insensitive remark. It's just that this story is important to me. Maybe that's all tied up with the battering my self-esteem took when I had to give up my career to move here. I know I can't walk away from it just because I'm afraid of something that might never happen."

"I know that's how you feel and I understand why,

but no story is worth getting yourself killed over. Let me do my job."

Amanda touched his arm, felt the taut muscle quiver beneath her touch. "I'm a professional, too, Donelli," she reminded him softly. "Let me do mine."

Their gazes clashed and held. Finally he sighed. "Do I have a choice?"

"Not really."

She saw the resigned look in his eyes even before he said, "Then let's go in and see what we can find. With any luck they won't have posted a guard, since the Atlanta police are convinced this was a suicide. I'd hate like hell to try and explain what we're doing here."

There was no guard. It took Donelli less than ten seconds to pick the flimsy lock, while Amanda held her breath and waited for some curious neighbor to peer into the corridor and catch them. For some reason she had never stopped to consider the fact that what they were doing was not exactly within the law. Okay, it was illegal. Having an almost official deputy with her didn't do much to reassure her, but she edged closer to him anyway.

"Back off, Amanda. You're in my light. It must be ninety-five degrees in this hallway and your teeth are chattering. What's wrong with you?" he asked.

"What if we get caught?"

"We'll be charged with breaking and entering."

It was not what she'd hoped to hear. "Terrific."

"Hey, this was your idea."

"You didn't have to go along with me."

"I beg your pardon."

"Oh, never mind. Just hurry up and get the door open."

With an obliging flourish, Donelli held it wide for her. Only when they were safely inside did her jittery nerves relax. She stood in the foyer and surveyed the living room.

The heat in Sarah Robbins's tightly closed apartment was oppressive, but the living room was as neat and tidy as Amanda had expected, despite the recent dusting for fingerprints by the police. Not an ashtray was out of place. Every magazine was precisely arranged on the shelf beneath the glass coffee table. There were stacks of *Gourmet*, *Bon Appetit*, *Southern Living*, *Good Housekeeping*, and *Family Circle* going back six months and a lone copy of *The New Yorker*.

In the bedroom Amanda suffered another attack of nerves. She kept her eyes carefully averted from the bed, where a chalk outline on the rumpled blue and beige flowered bedspread indicated the location of Sarah's body when it was discovered. The door to the closet was ajar and she opened it with the tip of one trembling finger. Sarah's wardrobe was organized rather obsessively by color to facilitate mixing and matching. There weren't many clothes, but those that hung on the padded hangers were of fine quality, another indication of Sarah's taste.

Amanda was suddenly saddened by the lack of personal memorabilia in the room. There were no photographs, no letters scattered about, no ticket stubs. In fact there was little evidence that anyone even lived in the apartment, aside from the size eight clothes and a small bottle of expensive French perfume on the bathroom counter.

"Doesn't look like she'd settled in, does it?" Donelli asked.

Amanda sank down on a dressing table bench and stared up at him. "It makes me want to cry."

"What does?"

"Thinking about that poor woman trying to start a new life here with a whole new identity."

Donelli sat down next to her. "Why the new identity, Amanda? Have you thought about that?"

Amanda bit her lip and considered it. It had been puzzling her on the drive over, too. "Maybe it was the only way she really felt she could start over."

"Or maybe it was the only way she could disguise her past. What do you really know about her? Maybe she was like that sick, obsessed broad in *Fatal Attraction*."

Amanda thought about the compulsive arrangement of Sarah's closet and had a moment's doubt. Then she shook her head. "No way. You can dismiss my instincts if you want to, Donelli, but I liked her. I empathized with her."

"And you don't empathize with murderers?"

"None that I've known of."

"Let me tell you what I think. I think she was holding back. When I interviewed her at the store, she certainly didn't admit to having known Chef Maurice before. Did she tell you?"

"No."

"Maybe there was more she chose not to tell us."

Amanda remembered Sarah's curtailed confidences, the odd tone of the suicide note. "Maybe so," she conceded. "But I can't help feeling she was a victim long before she died. She was down here with no friends. She must have been incredibly lonely. Then she heard that her ex-lover was coming to town."

"She *heard* he was coming to Atlanta. She manipulated the rest."

"Even so, it must have turned her whole world upside down all over again. Even though she'd tried to make a new life for herself, she still loved this man. For a while—a few days, maybe a couple of weeks—she had hope that she could get him back. Maybe he even promised her a reconciliation. Then he died and she had nothing."

"She had her life," Donelli reminded her. "That's pretty precious, but she made the decision to take it."

Amanda waved aside the argument. "Oh, come on now. You don't believe she made that decision any more than I do. If you did, you wouldn't be so worried about me."

"Okay. I'll concede that it doesn't add up, but there's no concrete evidence that this was anything other than a suicide. The note was pretty clear about her intentions. I'll say it again: For all we know she could have killed the chef herself, then been filled with such remorse that she didn't want to go on living."

"You say the note was clear. How do you even know she wrote it? Was it in her handwriting?"

"The Atlanta police seem to think it was."

"Oh, please. Is that good enough for you? What does your gut tell you?"

"My gut feelings won't hold up in court."

"No one's on trial yet. Come on, Donelli. You're an

experienced cop. You must have some instincts about this."

"Okay. You're right. It's just possible that someone murdered her because they thought she might know something," he answered reluctantly. "They could have faked the note or forced her to write it. They *could have*," he emphasized.

Amanda nodded in satisfaction. "I agree. So what do we do about it?"

"We keep looking for answers."

"Right. You keep checking in here. I'll go back through the rest of the apartment."

"You must be some sort of a witch, Amanda. Not only did I break into this place for you, but now you've got me tampering with evidence."

"We are not tampering. We're looking."

"Keep that in mind. Don't . . ."

"I know. I know. Don't touch anything. I'm not stupid, Donelli."

He threw up his hands. Unexpected laughter danced in his eyes. "Did I say that?"

"You didn't have to. It was written all over your face," she said as she stomped off in indignation.

The kitchen was a surprise. Not only was it exceptionally large for an apartment of this size, but also in sharp contrast to the rest of the place, it was a mess. Dishes and pots and pans were stacked haphazardly in the sink. The Formica counters were dusted with flour. It looked a little like the aftermath of a child's first attempt at making a Mother's Day breakfast. A nearly empty bottle of champagne was still on the table, the pale liquid devoid of bubbles. Chef Maurice's latest cookbook lay open beside the stove, the book's pages turned to a tantalizing recipe for Veal Bordelaise.

Amanda immediately imagined Sarah excitedly preparing a celebratory dinner for two, her hopes for the future pinned on this one evening with her former lover. Had they laughed together as they recalled old times? Had they danced perhaps? Had they made love in a tangle of sheets and heated flesh? Or had the dream's fragile bubble burst, leaving a woman who'd been scorned for the second time, a woman angry enough to seek revenge?

Amanda dismissed that final scenario. She recalled Sarah's tear-filled eyes as Chef Maurice lay dead behind her. Then she made herself a promise on the spot. "I'm going to find out who did this, Sarah. I'm going to find out just as much for you, as I am for me."

She began making a methodical search of the cheerful room, not sure just what she was looking for. For some reason she kept returning to the cookbook. It was as if beyond the tangible evidence it provided of the link between Sarah and the chef, she thought it might also offer a clue about their deaths. She wondered if Sarah had Chef Maurice's earlier volumes.

Using a napkin to open the cupboard doors, she scanned the contents until she came upon the shelf on which Sarah kept her cookbooks. There were more than a dozen of them, including two more by her former lover.

One by one Amanda took them out and examined them. Only after she'd removed what she thought was the last book did she discover yet another one. A well-used volume, its pages marred by greasy fingerprints and splattered ingredients, it had been tucked away out of sight. Written by Jean-Claude Meunier, its placement behind the others struck Amanda as decidedly odd. It was as though Sarah had been trying to hide the book from Chef Maurice, as if she feared he might feel betrayed by her obvious devotion to one of his competitors.

She removed the book and skimmed its contents, amused by the man's Gallic charm evidenced by his witty introductions to each section. Closing the book several minutes later, she noticed the author's picture on the back cover and gasped, immediately struck by the man's familiarity. The eyes were dark and brooding, the hair sparse, the face thin, the slightly disproportionate nose distinctive. A frisson of excitement rippled down her back.

"He was there. I know it," she murmured, thankful that Donelli was still in the other room. She could hardly wait to put the book back in its place, wrap things up here, and get back to the newspaper where she could go through Larry's prints from the murder scene. If she was right, if Jean-Claude had been in the crowd on the day Chef Maurice died, he could well be the murderer. At the very least, he might have more vital information that could help the investigation.

After a moment's indecision she decided not to share the clue with Donelli. Not right away, anyway. The big problem was going to be getting him to take her back home before brunch without arousing his suspicions.

Listening closely for his footsteps, she picked up the

phone with an oven mitt to avoid fingerprints and hur-
riedly dialed Larry's number.

"Yeah. Hello," the photographer said, his voice rough
and impatient. She could hear the televised baseball
game in the background and winced.

"Larry, it's me. Amanda."

"Why are you whispering? I can hardly hear you."

"Just be quiet and listen closely. I want you to meet
me at the office in two hours. I need to see prints of
everything you shot the day Chef Maurice died."

"Oscar already has all the good stuff."

"I'm not looking for a Pulitzer Prize-winning shot. I
need to ID somebody who was in the crowd that day."

"Amanda, you know I'd do anything for you, but it's
Sunday afternoon. It must be ninety degrees outside.
I'm sitting here in my nice air-conditioned apartment
with a beer in my hand. The Braves are playing a
double-header against the Dodgers. Don't ask me to
give up heaven for that closet Oscar likes to pretend is a
darkroom."

"Larry, please. It could be important."

"I must have shot a dozen rolls of film that afternoon.
Please, tell me you don't want me to do prints of everything."

She was beginning to hear the defeat in his voice.
"Just contact sheets. That's all I need. Maybe one
blowup, if I find what I'm looking for."

"You'll owe me dinner and I don't come cheap."

"Fine. Anything. Just meet me there."

She hung up before he could change his mind.

"Who were you talking to?"

Amanda jumped guiltily. "Talking? Was I talking? It

must have been to myself. Sometimes I do that, don't you?"

"Sometimes. But usually I don't pause and wait for answers. Who was it, Amanda?"

"The paper. I had to check in. Oscar thought he might have an assignment for me today and I'd forgotten all about it until a few minutes ago."

Donelli looked skeptical. "I wouldn't think Oscar would work on Sunday."

"He doesn't usually, but he didn't have time to do all the assignments for the week on Friday, so he asked me to call in today. Really," she swore. "That's all it was. I even called collect."

"If you say so, Amanda. Did you find anything in here?"

"Not really. Apparently Sarah had fixed a big dinner for the chef before he died."

"What makes you think it was for the chef? That would have been at least ten days ago. We don't have the coroner's report yet, but the guess is that she's only been dead for forty-eight hours or so. Did Sarah strike you as the type to leave dishes in her sink for a week?"

Amanda's eyes widened. "Why, no. I never even thought of that. That's very good, Donelli."

"Thank you," he said dryly. "Now that you've realized that I'm not totally inept, perhaps you'll leave the investigating to me."

"For the moment," she said agreeably.

The startled expression in Donelli's dark brown eyes was worth what it cost her to give in. Temporarily, anyway.

CHAPTER
Five

AS soon as they were back on the road, Donelli swung the car toward downtown. Amanda sensed that any attempt to dissuade him from brunch was doomed to failure. He was already suspicious about the phone call. If she openly displayed a sudden rush to leave Atlanta, it would convince him that she was up to no good. He might very well insist on going to the paper with her.

"Why don't we eat at that place you mentioned earlier?" she suggested, hoping at least to get them pointed toward home. She could just imagine what Larry's mood would be if she were very late.

"The one on the highway? Why would you want to go there when we're already in Atlanta? I thought we'd try the Hyatt. We can grab a little food, ask a few questions."

"Questions?" Her demeanor immediately brightened at the prospect. She'd buy an extra bottle of wine to go with the dinner she'd promised Larry. "Who do you plan to see?"

"That was the place where the chef stayed before he died. Maybe the desk clerk or a maid will remember something. Could be he had a late-night visitor or maybe someone left a note at the desk. I have a few more things I'd like to discuss with Webster, too."

"Come to think of it, so do I," Amanda said without thinking.

Donelli looked at her sharply. "Like what?"

"You first."

To her astonishment he answered. "I want some more details on how this stopover at Bobby Ray's was arranged. What about you?"

"When I talked to colleagues in New York, I heard some rumors I'd like to check out."

"Such as?"

"There were a couple of items in the New York gossip columns a few weeks back about arguments that Chef Maurice and Webster had been having all over town. One columnist reported that Webster was likely to be out of a job before the end of the tour."

Donelli slammed on the brakes and stared at her. "Amanda! Why the hell didn't you tell me that the minute you heard it?"

"Frankly, I didn't think it was all that important."

"A man the chef was about to fire has access to the substance that was used to kill him and you don't think it's important?"

His incredulity irritated her. Guilt only exacerbated the reaction. "Killing the chef wasn't going to help Jonathan Webster. He needed the job," she explained patiently.

"Thank you, Miss Marple. From now on, will you just give me the evidence and let me decide if it's important? Are there any other tidbits you haven't passed along?"

She thought about Jean-Claude, felt another momentary pang of guilt, and shook her head. She didn't trust herself to speak.

When they reached the hotel, Donelli reminded her at least half a dozen times to let him question Jonathan Webster. "You just sit there and nibble on your strawberries, okay?"

"If I think of a really terrific question, can I scribble it on a piece of paper and pass it to you?" she asked sarcastically.

To her satisfaction, now Donelli seemed to be grinding his teeth. "If it's a really terrific question, you can ask it yourself, Amanda."

Jonathan Webster actually seemed delighted to hear from them. He agreed to meet them in the coffee shop in fifteen minutes and to bring a copy of Chef Maurice's tour itinerary with him. He made it down in five. His eyes were red-rimmed and bleary. Amanda suspected he had replenished his supply of vodka several times since they'd last seen him.

"How much longer am I going to have to wait around in this godforsaken town?" he asked as soon as he was seated, their order taken, and the waitress had brought his coffee. His hand shook as he spooned in two scoops of sugar. His question was one Amanda herself had asked often.

"As long as it takes," Donelli responded. "You might be able to speed things up by answering a few more questions."

"Ask away. I figured this wasn't a social call."

"Were you on good terms with the chef the last few weeks?" Donelli inquired bluntly.

Jonathan Webster smiled wearily. "I should have known a couple of New Yorkers like you two would hear about those items sooner or later. We'd had fights, yes."

"What about?"

"I'm not sure the subject matter's important."

"How about letting me decide that," Donelli suggested.

"Off the record?" he asked with a pointed look at Amanda. Donelli stared at her too.

She sighed and put down her pen. "Off the record."

"Chef Maurice was a stubborn, opinionated man. He might have known how to make the perfect white sauce, but he didn't know the first thing about public relations. His agency hired me because they didn't trust him to make this tour alone. They figured he'd try to seduce some teenager who fell for his croissants and they'd have a nasty scandal on their hands. He didn't appreciate my meddling in his personal life. I couldn't very well tell the columnists that when they called. No comment seemed the diplomatic way to go."

"Was he going to fire you?"

"I'm sure he wanted to, but the agency was paying me. He was stuck with me until the tour ended. It was the one thing the agency wouldn't give in to him about. They had a big investment in him. I never heard for sure, but I think one of the people there had been an original backer. At any rate, they weren't about to take a chance on him making some stupid mistake with some bimbo and blowing the whole thing."

"Did you know about Sarah Robbins?"

"You mean that she had a thing for the chef? Sure, I knew. All you had to do was watch the lady when she talked about him. You could see it in her eyes. There were a hundred women just like her in every city."

"Did Chef Maurice ever tell you that he actually knew her?"

Amanda watched Jonathan Webster closely. There was genuine astonishment in his eyes. "He knew her? He never said a word to me about it. Neither did she, for that matter."

"Were you with him when he arrived for the demonstration?"

"Of course." He paused thoughtfully. "No, wait a minute. We came together in the limo, but I had to make some final arrangements with the driver. He went into the store without me."

"So you don't know if he greeted her like an old friend."

"No. By the time I got up there, they were talking like old friends, but that's just the way he was with women. I didn't think there was anything special about this one."

"Was there any other time during the Atlanta stop that they could have gotten together without your knowing about it?"

"Possible, but not likely. I'd tipped half the bellmen on the night shift to let me know if he tried to sneak out in the middle of the night."

"Who made the decision to do the demonstration at Johnson and Watkins? I'm looking at the original itinerary here and it wasn't on it."

"No, now that you mention it, it wasn't. I got a call from New York to add it. It meant changing a couple of things around and I could tell they weren't happy about it."

"Did they say it was the chef's idea?"

"No. I guess I just assumed it was. I didn't figure there was anybody down here except him with enough clout to get them to disrupt the schedule like that."

"Who would be able to tell us exactly how it was arranged?"

"Tina Whitehead. She's the head of the agency. She handled the chef's account personally, if you get my meaning."

Donelli and Amanda exchanged looks. Jonathan Webster's meaning was all too clear. Chef Maurice's well-publicized charm was obviously based on fact. It apparently had been fatal as well.

They wrapped up the interview quickly after that. When Webster left the table, Donelli looked at Amanda. "Well, what do you think?"

"I think we're missing something important. I wonder if the bellhops were bribed by the chef, too. It would explain how he might have slipped out of here without Webster knowing."

"I think we'll have to come back at night to find out. We'd be wasting our time with the day shift. According to this schedule, there weren't any breaks during the day. Whoever did the planning of the itinerary wanted to be sure the chef had as little time as possible to get himself in trouble."

"Tina Whitehead," Amanda deduced.

"Makes sense to me. I think it's time to get back home and make a few calls to see how close these two really were. I want to check in with Bobby Ray, too. He's anxious to hear how the investigation is coming."

This new lead served Amanda's purposes very well. It kept Donelli from noticing that she was in just as much of a hurry as he was to get home.

It was nearly six o'clock by the time she reached the newspaper office. Though it was still daylight outside, the layer of dirt that had accumulated on the window prevented any sunlight from penetrating. The room was already in gloomy shadows. Larry was leaning back in Oscar's chair, eyes closed, his size eleven sneakers propped on the desk, a scowl on his face. He didn't acknowledge Amanda's arrival by so much as the twitch of an eyelid.

Larry was only twenty-one years old and six months out of college, but, she decided, he was already showing signs of developing Oscar's grumpy temperament.

"Sorry I'm late," Amanda said cheerily. "It couldn't be helped."

There was a low rumble of disbelief. One eye opened to peer at her. "Two hours, Amanda. That's what you promised. May I point out that the two hours were up at precisely three twenty-two P.M. At three twenty-seven the Braves' third baseman hit a bases-loaded homer and I missed it."

"If you missed it, how do you know about it?"

"I was listening to the radio in the darkroom."

"Then you didn't miss it, did you?" She swept past him and dumped her purse on her desk, catching the cherry jelly bean that rolled out and popping it into her mouth. Larry rearranged his lanky frame to a standing posture and stalked after her. It was a little like being shadowed by a pro basketball player.

"Just hearing about it is not the same, Amanda. You have to actually see it to experience it. This better be good or you can start preparing yourself to explain to Oscar why I'm turning in four hours of overtime this week."

"Forget the overtime. If we break this case before the police do, Oscar will give us a bonus. We'll win national journalistic recognition. Our friends will be awed and amazed." Donelli, she thought with the first tiny twinge of regret, would be furious.

There was another snort of derision from Larry. "If you don't mind, I think I'll just hold out for the overtime. It's a sure thing."

"Tell me that again, after you've heard what I found out in Atlanta today."

Despite himself, Larry's eyes sparked with interest, but he managed a bored tone. "What?"

"Bring me those contact sheets and we'll talk about it."

"Tell me first."

"I'd rather show you."

Larry seemed to ponder whether it was worth it to argue the point, but he finally gave in. He cleared a space and spread the black and white prints out on the desk. "What are we looking for?"

"Not what. Who. Give me that magnifying glass."

Amanda peered at each tiny 35 mm photo. There were thirty-six exposures per contact sheet and by the time she reached the twelfth sheet, her eyes were strained and bleary. Her frustration was mounting as well. She tossed the final print aside, then swept the scattered sheets back into a pile and started all over again.

"Dammit, he has to be here. Turn on the overhead lights, Larry. It's darker than midnight in here."

Larry flipped a switch and the equivalent of four 25-watt bulbs cast a dim glow on the contact sheets. Oscar's ideas about electricity bordered on the parsimonious.

"Who has to be there?" Larry asked, coming back to peer over her shoulder.

"Jean-Claude Meunier."

"Who the hell is he?"

"If my hunch is right, he could be our murderer."

Once more she squinted, studying each photo through the magnifying glass. She tried not to notice that Larry was breathing in her ear. Suddenly her heart began to pound and a rush of adrenaline swept through her. It had nothing to do with Larry's proximity.

"Bingo!" she said triumphantly.

"You found him?"

"Big as life. I don't know how I missed that nose the first time around."

"Let me see." Larry squinted at the tiny picture.

"Hey, yeah, I remember him now. I talked to the guy. He asked me about the shots I'd taken."

"He what?" She grabbed hold of Larry's arm.

He yelped. "Hey, watch it!"

She let go. "Sorry. What did he ask you?"

"He wanted to know if I'd taken crowd shots or if I'd just taken pictures of the demonstration. I thought it was a little peculiar to be asking about crowd shots with a dead chef center stage."

Amanda's excitement grew and Larry cautiously backed up a step.

"Don't you see?" she exclaimed. "He was afraid of just this."

"Afraid of what? He didn't act afraid, just a little wired. I figured he was just some nervous little Frenchman."

"He was nervous all right. You'd be nervous too, if you'd just knocked off your competition in plain sight of a newspaper photographer."

"Okay, so we can place this Jean-Claude guy at the scene. So what? We didn't catch him doctoring the almond extract. I've watched a lot of old 'Perry Mason' reruns. I don't think that's enough to hold up in court."

"Maybe not, but that picture proves he had the opportunity to do it."

"Great. By that standard, you and I had the opportunity, too. What about motive? Did this guy have it in for Chef Maurice?"

Amanda frowned. "I'm not so sure about that yet. Maybe there was some sort of professional rivalry. Sarah said something about jealousy. Maybe that's what she meant. I'd give anything for a decent library in this office. The last time Oscar filed a clipping was Pearl Harbor Day."

"As long as you're dreaming impossible dreams, you might as well wish for a computer hookup to the library at *The New York Times* or *The Washington Post*. Barring that, what are you going to do?"

She picked up her purse. "I'm going back to Atlanta."

"At this hour?"

"It's only eight o'clock, for heaven's sake. I'll be there in an hour or so. Besides, unlike this place, real newspapers don't shut down at six. Somebody who can let me into the *Constitution*'s files will be working."

"Couldn't you just call?"

"I don't want to tip them off about what I'm working on."

"Okay. If you're going, I'm coming with you."

"Forget it, Larry. Go on back home and watch your baseball game."

"Use me and lose me, is that it? Not nice, Amanda. Besides, you know you hate driving on these country roads alone after dark. You told me it gives you the creeps."

It was actually a very persuasive argument, but Amanda turned it down regretfully. "That doesn't mean I have to have a bodyguard."

"Then let's pretend I'm just a curious colleague who won't be able to sleep a wink until I know what's going on."

Because he seemed to be dogging her footsteps anyway, Amanda finally gave in. Every minute she spent arguing with Larry was costing her precious time. She figured it wouldn't take Donelli all that long to catch on to what she was doing, and when he did he was going to be mad as hell. His anger was likely to cut back considerably on the amount of time she had to conduct independent research.

"Let's go," she said.

"I'm right behind you," Larry said as they stepped out into the darkening street.

"How gallant."

It was nearly midnight when Amanda finally conceded that she'd dragged the two of them on a wild-goose chase. She and Larry were surrounded by dusty old files. She sneezed and threw the last of the clips down in disgust.

"Nothing. Nothing but a handful of gushing profiles and some book reviews. There's not one damn thing here to suggest that Jean-Claude had a motive to kill Chef Maurice. If there was a rivalry, they hid it in public. I can't even tell for certain if they ever met."

"But your instincts are still telling you he did it," Larry said.

"Yes, but why? Do you suppose our dead chef once stole a recipe from Jean-Claude?"

"That hardly seems like a reason to murder the guy."

"Maybe it was his favorite recipe."

"Amanda!"

"I know," she said, rubbing her tired eyes. "I can't help it. I'm exhausted and frustrated. I was so sure we were going to turn up something. This is the only solid theory I've been able to come up with."

"Come on. I'll buy you a drink and take you home."

"No drink. I just want to get home and get to bed. That dinner I owe you will have to wait."

"No problem. I know you're good for it. I'll just camp out on your doorstep on payday."

Larry dropped her off at her car and waited until she was safely inside before driving away. Amanda drove home, her mind filled with variations of her original theory. As soon as she got there, she poured herself a glass of iced tea, added a sprig of mint, and then took the drink to the front porch. She settled herself in her favorite rocking chair and let the night sounds surround her. Though she tried to concentrate on the investigation, it was Donelli's face that kept coming to mind. She sighed and closed her eyes.

"Go away, Donelli," she grumbled under her breath. As she might have expected, he paid no attention to her. He plagued her thoughts with images of the disappointed look he'd have in his eyes when he discovered what she'd been up to. For some reason it was becoming increasingly important that Donelli think well of her. For a woman who'd sworn off romance, especially a romance that might keep her in Georgia one second longer than necessary, it was a disturbing turn of events.

"Okay. Okay. I'll tell you what I've found," she said, then amended, "as soon as I've really found something."

The next morning she placed a call to Jean-Claude's publisher and was advised that she'd have to reach him through his agent. The address she was given was on Park Avenue. That told her all she needed to know about Aaron Leibowitz. He either came from old money or he had a stable of very successful clients. Directory assistance provided the phone number.

She had to go through three secretaries just to get him on the line. He put her on hold for four minutes after she said hello and another ten minutes after she gave him her name. Once he settled at least half of his attention on her for three straight minutes, it took a flat-out bluff to get the information she wanted. She told him she wanted very much to do a free-lance feature for a national magazine. She was intentionally vague about which one, though Mr. Leibowitz just might have gathered from her hints that it was *Gourmet*.

Jean-Claude was in Miami, he said, instantly cooperative. He was on a cross-country tour to promote his own new cookbook. Although Aaron Leibowitz offered a glowing report on Jean-Claude's reception in each city, she thought she detected an undercurrent of false, PR-inspired enthusiasm in his remarks.

"Has Mr. Meunier been in Atlanta during this tour?"

"Of course. He was invited to participate in that chocolate lover's demonstration. I have a stack of clips in front of me right now. By all accounts his mousse was the hit of the show."

Amanda had seen those same clips. She thought his analysis was slightly exaggerated. One particularly unkind critic had said the recipe was "inspired to mediocrity." She supposed that a savvy agent would automatically leave off the last two words in his next press kit. Jean-Claude's *inspired* mousse would become world famous.

"Did he stay over after the event?" she asked.

"Perhaps just that one night, but I don't believe any

longer. Charlotte, bring me Jean-Claude's schedule. Hustle, honey, I don't want to keep the lady waiting. Yeah, here it is. He was scheduled to be in Savannah the next day, then Charleston the day after that. The only break he's had since the tour began has been in Miami. I expect him to be there until the end of the week. You want to go down there, honey, I could set it up."

"Thanks, but I'll have to get back to you on that. Do you happen to know if he was going to all the same cities as Chef Maurice?"

A muffled oath, then a lengthening silence met the question.

"Are you still there, Mr. Leibowitz?"

"Yes."

"Did you hear the question?"

"I heard it," he said warily, "but I have to wonder why you'd ask it? I thought you were interested in Jean-Claude."

"Oh, I am. I just thought perhaps if the two men were traveling the same circuit, they might be friends."

"Hardly." There was another pause. "Perhaps you haven't heard, but Chef Maurice is dead. I don't know much about it. There was only a small item in the paper."

"Yes, I'd heard," she said. Then she added quickly, "Thanks so much for your help. I will get back to you about that interview."

Five minutes later she had Jean-Claude on the phone. After dutifully raving about the reports of his success in Atlanta, she asked about the appearances in Savannah and Charleston.

"There was a last-minute cancellation in Savannah,"

he said sorrowfully. "Such a lovely city. I was sorry to miss it."

Amanda's pulse raced. "Who canceled?"

"I did. The influenza. *Terrible. Vraiment, terrible,*" he said, slipping into French. She wondered if he did that when he was nervous.

"Monsieur Meunier."

"Jean-Claude, *s'ils vous plait*. Please."

"Jean-Claude, are you familiar with an American chef, a Chef Maurice?"

There was no silence this time, nor any attempt to hide a reaction. She heard a hiss of anger, then an outpouring of French. Her college French hadn't prepared her for either the speed or the colorful vocabulary. "I'm sorry. I don't understand. Could you speak more slowly? In English?"

"He is, how you say, le fraud. A fake. He is nothing. Why would you ask that of me?"

"You do know him, then?"

"But, of course. From ze beginning. I taught him everything." He paused and caught his breath. *"Non.* I will not discuss. He is beneath me. I must go now."

The phone clicked emphatically and the line went dead.

"Well, well," Amanda murmured as she replaced the receiver. "It sounds as though there might have been a bad case of professional jealousy there, especially if the student's success surpassed the teacher's."

She shared her hunch with Oscar. "What do you think?"

"You think that's enough for him to murder the guy? I don't buy it. Sure, it eliminates the competition, but if you get thrown in jail yourself, it looks to me like you've played to a draw."

"Oscar, you have to let me check this out. I've got sources in New York who can help me, put me in touch with the right people. I think Leibowitz knows a lot more than he admitted, too. We've got national attention focused down here. You don't want Bobby Ray to mess it up, do you?"

"Your sudden concern for Bobby Ray does my old heart good, Amanda. It's nice you're beginning to feel some civic pride." He gestured toward her desk. "Pick up the phone and call anybody you want."

"You know you can work a story better in person, Oscar. You can see the look in their eyes, tell when they're lying."

"You try hearing the lies in their voices, why don't you? It'll be good practice. I'm not forking out a thousand bucks so you can go up there, hang out in some fancy hotel and visit your pals."

"I'm not going on a visit. It's called an assignment, Oscar," she snapped. She studied his implacable expression, then threw up her hands. "Never mind. I'll call."

Twenty-four hours after she'd spoken with Jean-Claude and half a dozen people in New York, Amanda was driving home at dusk when a bullet crashed through the windshield of her brand new Toyota, just barely missing her twenty-eight-year-old head. It was not, she suspected, the act of someone who'd merely disliked her story on the upcoming cat show.

CHAPTER

Six

IT was the second shot that actually shattered the windshield. Terrified now, Amanda instinctively slammed on the brakes and threw her hands up in front of her face. She could feel shards of glass pricking her skin, then a warm dampness that she knew without looking was blood. Her stomach rolled over.

Apparently her foot had slipped from the brake to the accelerator because the next thing she knew the car was moving, hurtling forward. Without her hands on the wheel to guide it, the car skidded wildly toward the shoulder of the road. Flashes of trees blurred before her eyes and the scent of pine seemed to fill her senses. She hit the brakes as hard as she could. At the same time, she grabbed the steering wheel and wrenched it to the left just in time to prevent the car from rolling down an embankment. As the brakes caught, the whole car seemed to shake as violently as she did in the aftermath of the accident.

Switching off the ignition with a trembling hand, she slid down in the seat and waited for a third, more deadly shot. A cold trickle of perspiration ran between her shoulder blades. Her heart thundered. Whoever had shot twice already was most likely determined enough to try again.

Amanda wasn't sure how long she sat there, frozen by shock, waiting for the next bullet to strike, too numb to retreat to safety. Her pulse finally began to slow to a more normal rate. When enough time had passed, she realized that for now she had won a reprieve. She felt exactly the way she had in New York when she'd heard about the car bomb—stunned by the narrowness of her escape, relieved. Dear God, she had never felt such relief—then and now. Her eyes stung with unshed tears.

Before a new wave of hysteria could wash over her, she bit her lower lip and tried to recall every single detail about the incident. She was surprised by how little she remembered. Her powers of observation must have been dimmed by fear. No image of a car pulling up beside her came to mind, no suggestion of a sniper hiding alongside the road.

"Damn! Damn! Damn!" she muttered, continuing to curse her own inadequacy as a witness and the idiot who'd taken the shot at her, endangering not only her, but others.

But there had been no others. She remembered that much now. That's one reason the shot had been so terrifying. It had come from out of nowhere. She had seen no cars in the rearview mirror, nor had there been any immediately ahead of her on the winding country road. The marksman had chosen well—a lonely stretch of road, an hour when the traffic was especially light, a time consistent with her daily schedule. The realization of how carefully someone had planned the attack brought on a new wave of trembling, then a sharp, reviving anger.

When she finally felt steady enough to drive, she drove the remaining half mile home, then sat in the driveway, struck anew by a sense of danger, too frightened to go inside. As much as she had resented moving here, she had always loved the little house with its crooked porch and wide-open, cheerful kitchen. It was such a contrast to the dark, cramped apartment she and Mack had paid three times as much to rent in New York. Now this charming old house loomed ominously in the twilight shadows, a haven for who knew what new terrors.

Finally, infuriated by the sniper's hold on her, she drew in a deep breath and stormed into the house, slamming the kitchen door behind her. The resounding crash was both a warning to any intruder and reassurance to her that her control was returning.

Without pausing to wipe away the streaks of blood on her face and arms, she instinctively picked up the phone and called Donelli. She wasted no time on amenities.

"This is Amanda. Can you get over to my place right away?"

Either he thought this was his lucky night or he heard the fury in her voice. At any rate, he didn't ask questions.

"I'll be there in ten minutes."

She was sitting at the kitchen table when he burst through the door. Before he could even start a lecture about the fact that she'd left the backdoor unlocked, she said, "Did you happen to notice my car on your way in?"

His gaze narrowed as he took in the tall, half-empty glass of Scotch she held tightly in both hands, her ashen complexion, the trail of blood on her face and arms, and the edge of hysteria in her voice.

His face turned pale and his voice dropped to a gentle, soothing pitch she'd never heard before. "What happened?"

"Just go and look at it."

He hesitated, his eyes filled with concern. "Will you be okay?"

"I should be able to survive the next five minutes without your company, if that's what you mean."

He was gone less than three minutes. She timed him by the second hand on her watch.

His eyes blazed and there were the familiar tiny white lines of tension around his lips when he came in, as if he were waging a tremendous battle to stay calm. It was definitely not his natural state. The restrained anger came out in his tone and the rephrasing of his original question.

"What the hell happened?"

"You're the detective. I thought you said guns weren't our killer's style."

"Don't get cute with me, Amanda. Just spill the details. Are you okay?" He found a paper towel over the sink, dampened it and knelt beside her, dabbing gently at the dried blood.

"A few cuts from the glass," she said, her voice suddenly shaky. She met his disbelieving gaze and tried a wavery smile. "That's all. I swear. I'm a little short on details, though, Donelli. Someone used my windshield for target practice when I was driving home about a half hour ago. It could have been an innocent mistake. Just some guy practicing for deer hunting season or maybe some kids on a spree. Maybe it wasn't even a bullet. Maybe they were just throwing rocks. I hear that happens a lot in a major metropolitan area."

He ignored the sarcastic tone and focused on the substance of her remark. "Is that what you really think happened?"

Suddenly drained and tired of the effort to appear brave and strong, she put down the glass and admitted somewhat wistfully, "It's what I'd like to believe."

"It wasn't a rock, Amanda." His voice was very soft. He held out a bullet. It sat in the roughened palm of his hand looking incredibly small and innocent for something that could have been so deadly. "I dug this out of the upholstery in the backseat. I'm going to call Bobby Ray right now and tell him to send it to Atlanta for a ballistics analysis."

"Don't." Amanda stared at the bullet and drew in a shaky breath, not sure why she felt so certain that involving Bobby Ray would be a mistake. If he knew, then Oscar would find out about it and he'd tell Larry. The next thing she knew, everyone would be hovering over her, worrying about her every move.

Donelli stood up and began to pace. She saw the warmth and concern in his eyes. Despite her best intentions, tears spilled down her cheeks. He was back at her side in an instant, pulling her out of the chair and into his arms. She found herself sobbing so hard she soaked the front of his shirt. His arms were tight around her and he was murmuring soothing little sounds. She listened closely just to make sure he wasn't muttering curses, but it seemed he was a gentleman, after all. He didn't say he'd told her so.

"Oh, Amanda, don't cry. It makes me crazy to see a woman cry."

"I don't want to cry, Donelli," she said and hiccuped. "I'm just so mad."

"And scared."

"I am not . . ." She hiccuped again. "Not scared."

"Okay. Okay," he soothed. "Just try to tell me exactly what happened. Where were you when the bullet hit?"

The question brought on another flood of tears. Donelli scooped her into his arms and carried her into the living room. He sat down in an overstuffed armchair and settled her on his lap. She supposed it was not exactly a professional way of conducting a police interrogation, but to her distress, if not entirely to her surprise, she found that she liked it very much. After Mack, she hadn't planned on liking men in general for some time to come. After dealing with Donelli for the last few days, she especially hadn't planned on liking him. Maybe it was just nerves. Maybe any strong arms would have done.

To her amazement, however, something about Donelli had apparently gotten to her. She had reacted to the shooting by calling him instinctively—not Oscar, not Larry, not even Mack, whose abilities in a crisis had been proven in New York. The call was not made entirely due to Donelli's professional capabilities, either, though through all the bickering and competitiveness, she'd begun to respect him as a detective. He had all the right, street-wise instincts. He asked all the right questions. But there was a certain gentleness and compassion in him that had softened the hard edges she'd come to expect in New York cops. Until now, she hadn't taken time to examine his good points, but apparently her subconscious—or her hormones—had done it for her. For a macho detective, Donelli just might not be all bad.

"Now will you cooperate?" he asked patiently.

"Are you still referring to the case?" she inquired, probably a little too hopefully.

He grinned. "For the moment, Amanda."

She quickly changed directions. "I suppose you believe my theory now."

"More important, I suppose you believe mine. This isn't some kid's game."

So much for gentlemanliness. He was going to rub it in. "Okay, Donelli. I admit it. You were right. Partially. We can no longer assume even for the sake of argument that Sarah Robbins killed Chef Maurice and then herself. If she had, the whole thing should have ended." She perked up and gave him a jaunty smile. "Unless you'd like me to believe that she's coming back from the dead to get me. It would make a terrific angle for the story."

"No. I'll concede that point."

"Thank you."

"You're welcome. Just one thing."

"What's that?"

"What have you been doing since we left Atlanta yesterday?"

"My laundry. I went in to work. Picked up a few groceries," she said cheerfully. "That's about it."

"I don't believe you. What else, Amanda?"

"I madeafewphonecalls," she mumbled into his shoulder.

"I didn't quite catch all of that."

"I made a few phone calls."

"More," he demanded.

Reluctantly, she told him about Jean-Claude. "I picked up on something else while I was calling around. Apparently Chef Maurice does have family, a brother. No one seems to know where to find him, though. Don't you think it's a little strange that he hasn't shown up to claim the body or something? Surely he knows about the death. It's been on TV and probably in every paper."

"Let's stick with Jean-Claude for the moment. We can try to track down the brother later. You're sure this Jean-Claude was in the crowd that day?"

She glowered at him.

"Okay. He was there. And your theory is that he was driven to madness by Chef Maurice's current acclaim and decided to rid himself of the competition?"

"Well, it makes sense, doesn't it? Jean-Claude was the leading French cooking expert in the country until Chef Maurice came along and got a hit television show. Jean-Claude's popularity is fading now. Boeuf bourguignon is boeuf bourguignon, but Jean-Claude just couldn't compete with those debonair good looks of Chef Maurice."

"You had the hots for the chef?"

Amanda gave him a disgusted look. "Not me, but

millions of other women did. Jonathan Webster told you that much."

"Maybe Jean-Claude did, too."

"Don't be crude."

"It was just a theory."

"If that's your idea of a theory, it's a good thing you left Brooklyn."

"In Brooklyn it would probably have been true."

"Let's put Jean-Claude on the back burner for a minute, so to speak. Did you track down Tina Whitehead?"

"Oh, I tracked her down all right," he said, his disgust apparent. "She was recovering from her grief at some estate on Long Island."

"What's so odd about that? You sound as though you disapprove. Lots of executives have estates on Long Island."

"Do most of them entertain lavishly within days of the death of a close friend?"

"How do you know she was entertaining?"

"You mean aside from the roars of laughter and the breaking of crystal I could hear in the background?"

"Circumstantial," Amanda said wisely. "It could have been a video."

"Of what? The chariot race in *Ben Hur* didn't create that much commotion."

"Maybe it was *Police Academy*."

Donelli didn't seem to appreciate the humor in the remark. "Okay," she said contritely. "So what's your point?"

"That Tina Whitehead's distress did not seem in proportion to her alleged personal relationship with the chef."

"Maybe that relationship was so much PR hype."

"No, I'm inclined to believe Webster's version. In fact, I'll take it one step further. I think she hired him specifically to protect her personal—not her business— interest in Chef Maurice."

"So now you think she killed the chef when she found out he'd escaped his baby-sitter? Wouldn't it have made more sense to kill Webster? At least with the chef alive, she stood to make some money."

"There are more important things than money. You should know that, Amanda. Isn't that what brought you to Georgia?"

"I'd rather not discuss what brought me to Georgia, thank you very much. And if that's considered sufficient motive for murder, then why is Mack still alive and well in Athens?"

Donelli gave her a particularly knowing smirk. "I think I'll let you figure that one out for yourself, Amanda."

Amanda considered driving an elbow into his stomach, but settled instead for asking, "So, what now, hot-shot?"

"You mean you don't have a plan?" He worked at appearing stunned.

"No, actually I thought I'd leave that up to you," she said with suitable humility.

He grinned in satisfaction. "It's about time."

Amanda shifted positions on Donelli's lap. Suddenly she felt the muscles in his shoulders tense.

"Umm, Amanda." There was a definite tightness in his voice.

She met his gaze evenly, glanced down at the curve of

his lips, then back to his eyes and waited. He swallowed hard.

"Oh, hell," he muttered.

His fingers tangled in her hair so slowly that it created aching anticipation. He drew her head lower. Lips that caressed like satin, then burned with passion's flame, took hers again and again until her breath came in quick, shallow gasps. There were tender, tentative kisses, then hard, hungry possessions that made her heart pound and sent her senses reeling. Arousal for both of them was swift, urgent, undeniable, yet there was no more than the kisses between them. His hands never touched her breasts, though they ached for him to. Her fingers never left his cheeks, though she wanted to explore.

When he lifted her from his lap at last and resettled her in the chair, she felt oddly bereft. His gaze lingered where only moments before his lips had inflamed. His thumb gently traced her kiss-swollen mouth and a soft smile lit his features.

"Night, angel," he said and left her.

Amanda stared after him, still shaken. She touched her plundered lips and felt again an echo of that sweet shaft of pleasure that had surprised, then intoxicated her.

"Oh, hell," she whispered.

CHAPTER
Seven

DESPITE her hint of sudden docility to Donelli the night before, there was one other tiny little thing Amanda thought she ought to check out personally.

At precisely 10:01 the next morning, after dropping her damaged car at a repair shop and picking up a rental, she rode the escalator back to the third floor of Bobby Ray's department store. It was the first time she'd been back since the day Chef Maurice had died so dramatically.

Naturally the makeshift stage was gone. The electric can opener sale had ended. Now sets of plastic glasses with bright pink flamingos on them had been marked down for an end-of-summer clearance—in July. Did the store honestly think people were already thinking about fall? It was one of those weird merchandising concepts that had always puzzled Amanda. Did anyone really buy wool clothes when it was ninety-seven degrees outside? Or bathing suits when it was thirty-two?

Picking up a package of four glasses as a cover for her real purpose, she looked around the deserted cookware department for some sign of a sales clerk. She was hoping to find someone who might have known Sarah Robbins's mood and actions over the last few days of her life.

She finally spotted a pregnant teenager rearranging the table of kitchen gadgets. The girl was staring at a garlic press as if she didn't know quite what to make of it. Amanda walked up behind her.

"Excuse me."

The girl jumped several inches, whirled around, and knocked half the display on the floor with a noisy clatter. She blushed a fiery red all the way to the dark roots of her blond hair. She began scooping up the plastic egg slicers, the little metal meat mallets, the cheese slicers, and the serrated grapefruit spoons. Amanda bent to help her.

"Oh, dear. I'm terribly sorry," she apologized, revising her guess of the clerk's age upward by a couple of years. She was probably in her early twenties. It was the lack of makeup and the ponytail that had made her appear younger.

"I didn't mean to startle you," Amanda said.

The clerk smiled, transforming her face. No longer plain, her expression became lively and her personality took on the eager friendliness of a puppy. She carelessly dumped a handful of gadgets helter-skelter back on the table.

"It's okay," she said with an appealing drawl. "I'm just really clumsy. That's why they took me out of the china department. I broke three place settings of Noritake and one of those wineglasses that cost half a week's salary. Some kind of crystal."

"Waterford?"

"Yeah. I think that was it. I always buy my wineglasses from K-Mart. Jimmy Joe says we might as well, seeing as how the wine's not fancy either. We buy it by the jug in the supermarket."

"It sounds like Jimmy Joe is a pragmatic man."

She stared at Amanda blankly. "A what?"

"A sensible, practical man."

The friendly smile reappeared. "That's Jimmy Joe all right. Mama says it's a good thing too, 'cause I ain't got a lick of sense."

Amanda refrained from comment. She found that she instinctively liked this girl and that she had no desire to join her mother in putting her down. "I wanted to buy these glasses. Could you help me?"

"Sure thing. That's what I'm here for."

She took the package and lumbered toward the cash register.

"So, tell me . . ." Amanda peered at the name tag. "Tell me, Sue Ellen, when did they move you into this department?"

"Oh, about six months ago, I reckon. I had seniority, you might say. That's why Mama was so mad when they brought in that Northern lady back in June and put her in charge. She said it was a clear-cut case of discrimination."

"Did you feel that way, too?"

"Maybe a little bit at first. Then I got to know her. That Ms. Robbins was mighty smart. She had lots of experience and she was always nice to me. Treated me like I was somebody. Asked my opinion about things. She wasn't like no boss I ever had before."

"It sounds as though you really liked her."

"I did," she said, a genuine note of sadness in her voice.

"Then maybe you wouldn't mind telling me a little more about her. I'm Amanda Roberts, a reporter for the *Gazette*."

Sue Ellen's expression brightened. "Oh, sure, I know you. You did that story about Chef Maurice dying and all."

"Yes, and now I'm doing a story about Ms. Robbins's death. It would really help if I could talk to someone who knew her."

Sue Ellen's eyes lit with excitement. "You mean you'd put my name in the paper and everything?"

"Absolutely."

"Oh, wow, wait 'til I tell Jimmy Joe and Mama. They're not gonna believe it. What did you want to know?"

"Anything you can remember about what she was like, how people around here felt about her."

"Well, now, not many folks around here got to know her. She was real private like." She shook her head sadly. "Sure did make me feel bad, when I heard what happened to her. Doesn't surprise me none, though. A lady like that killing herself. Mama says it's the sort of thing you have to expect from one of them fancy Yankee career women. Too much stress, if you ask me. A woman can't take all that stress the way a man can."

Amanda flinched, but decided against trying to educate Sue Ellen about women's liberation. It would not help her in this particular environment.

Sue Ellen's hand hovered over the cash register as her mind wandered. A dreamy expression came over her face. Amanda let the girl's thoughts roam, hoping she would inadvertently offer some extraordinary bit of information she didn't even know she possessed about Sarah Robbins.

"The week before that cooking demonstration, Ms. Robbins was real jittery," she said finally. "I thought maybe it was because she'd never handled anything like that before, but I asked her and she said, yes she had. She said she'd done a lot of them up North."

"Did she say where up North? Or what store?"

"She said the name of the store. I don't remember, though. I think it was that one that has the Thanksgiving parade on TV every year."

"Macy's?"

"Yeah, that's the one. I remember because we talked about those big balloons they always have in the parade. My little boy, Jimmy Joe Junior, he just loves those balloons."

"Did Ms. Robbins say if it was the store in Manhattan or one of the branches?"

"Not to me. Maybe personnel knows. They probably check stuff like that."

But had they checked Sarah Robbins's references or Sandra Reynolds's? Or had they simply been so delighted to find someone with merchandising experience from a major national retailer that they'd just accepted her at her word? Amanda wondered if that was something Bobby Ray would feel like sharing with her.

"How was Sarah on the day of the demonstration?"

"She was still real tense like. Not that she went around snapping at everybody or anything like that. She just didn't smile the way she usually did and nothing seemed to please her. I brought her some of Mama's special corn bread and she didn't even touch it."

"Did she do or say anything else that seemed strange to you around that time?"

"Strange? How do you mean?"

"Something that wasn't quite like her usual self, something that suggested why she was so upset?"

"Now that you mention it, I believe she did. Yes, that's right. It wasn't on the day of the demonstration, mind you, but one day I heard her yelling in her office. Wasn't like nothing I ever heard before from a refined lady like that. Surprised the dickens out of me that she'd be using the kind of talk I'm always getting on Jimmy Joe about using."

"Was she on the phone?"

"No, ma'am. She had some man in there and she was telling him off right and proper in language that would have made my Aunt Fannie Mae blush."

"When exactly was this, Sue Ellen?"

"Now let me just think a minute." She idly rubbed her swollen belly. "Seems to me like it was the day before the demonstration, 'cause I thought maybe it was just some detail that had gotten fouled up."

"Did you hear what she was saying?"

Sue Ellen looked shocked. "Why, no, ma'am. It ain't

polite to listen to other folks' conversations. I mean they were yelling loud and all, but I did my best not to pay any attention to what they was saying."

Amanda sighed in disappointment. "I don't suppose you saw the man either or recognized his voice?"

"No, ma'am." She rang up Amanda's purchase, gave her the change, and then put the glasses in a bag.

Amanda was ready to take the hideous glasses and leave, but then Sue Ellen said, "You know something, though. Now that I think about it and all, I just might have seen him the day of the demonstration. I'm not sayin' I did, but it could have been."

Amanda had to refrain from shaking the girl until the whole story came spilling out. Sue Ellen was not the sort of interview subject you rushed. She'd get all nervous and defensive if she really stopped to think about her words appearing in print. "What makes you think so?"

"Well, we were running around here like crazy the next morning. Ms. Robbins, she was worried that things wouldn't go like she planned, so she had us checking everything twice. Then all of a sudden she went real pale. I asked her if she was sick and she said no, but she was acting real funny. She walked over to this man and said something to him. Looked to me like they was arguin' about something, though they didn't raise their voices like they had the day before, so I can't be real sure it was the same one. He sort of smiled at her finally and left. He came back later, though. I saw him after . . . after, well, you know. After that chef died and all."

"He was here then? After the demonstration? You're absolutely sure?"

"Of course I'm sure. I've got a real good memory for faces. Why do you want to know all this anyway?"

Why, indeed. "I liked Sarah Robbins, too, Sue Ellen. I want to do anything I can to find out what really happened to her so that everyone will know the truth."

Sue Ellen looked puzzled. "Why, she committed suicide. That's what happened. I read it in the paper and then Bobby Ray, he came up here and talked to me about it. He said the same thing. Told me I shouldn't feel too bad, that Ms. Robbins had always spoken highly of me. It was nice of him to say that, seeing as how I could tell he was real upset himself. Then he told me I'd be in charge for now."

"Congratulations," Amanda said, not wanting to disillusion Sue Ellen just yet about Sarah's fate. "Would you mind doing something else for me? If I brought some pictures over here, do you think you could take a look at them and see if you recognize anyone?"

"You mean that man?"

"Yes, that man. It could be important."

"Why, sure," she said, pleased as punch about the recognition of her skills. "You just bring 'em over whenever you want. I'm here 'til the store closes."

"Thanks, Sue Ellen. I'll be back later this afternoon."

Amanda's thoughts tumbled like cottonweed in the wind as she walked slowly to the escalator. Sue Ellen just might hold the key to this entire case. But before she went back to the office for the contact sheets, Amanda wanted to stop by personnel and see what she could discover there.

The executive suite on the second floor opened off the dress department. The carpeting was a muted blue, the furniture French provincial in a polished pecan wood. The woman sitting at the receptionist's desk could have kept the German troops out of France in World War II.

She looked up as Amanda approached and lowered her unrimmed spectacles to the tip of her nose. "May I help you?"

Amanda introduced herself, causing the woman's frown to deepen. "I was hoping to speak to someone in charge of personnel."

"Why?"

The blunt question caught Amanda off guard. She had hoped to find some obliging young clerk on duty, someone like Sue Ellen, who would be impressed at the prospect of being interviewed and wouldn't think too carefully about any store rules. Miss Emma Lou Timmons not only knew the rules, but also she probably thought they were too lenient. For lack of anything better, she told her the same thing she'd told the sales clerk.

"I'm doing a story on Sarah Robbins's death and I was hoping to get a little background information," Amanda said, trying to make it all sound terribly innocuous.

Miss Timmons's prim mouth formed a little bow of displeasure. "I'm afraid that won't be possible. Our personnel records are very confidential. I'm afraid Mr. Johnson would have to approve any request to see them and he isn't here today. If you could come back next week, perhaps he could see you then."

"He's out for the entire week?"

"Yes. Now if you don't mind, I have work to do."

She pushed her glasses back in place with one finger and began typing. Amanda clearly had been dismissed.

Irritated by the abrupt dismissal and discouraged by the failure to get so much as a peek at Sarah's personnel file, she found herself muttering under her breath as she returned to the escalator and left the store.

In an attempt to pick up her spirits, she reminded herself about Sue Ellen's revelation. The morning had hardly been a total loss. It should take her a half hour to pick up the contact sheets and another half hour to get back to Bobby Ray's store. By mid-afternoon she could be well on her way to identifying the murderer.

She hadn't counted on Donelli.

He was sitting at her desk, a copy of the Atlanta morning paper draped across his chest. His eyes were closed, but she had a feeling that didn't mean she could sneak back out without getting caught. She resigned herself to a lengthy delay.

"Reading the competition, I see," she said, swiveling his chair away from her desk and pulling another one over for herself. He regarded her skeptically.

"You consider this your competition?" he said, reaching for her jar of jelly beans. Judging from the level of her supply, it was not the first grab he'd made. She'd have to make another urgent call this afternoon to order more.

"You're working for a twenty-eight-page weekly tabloid," he reminded her unkindly.

Amanda bristled with indignation. She snatched the jar out of his reach. "That doesn't mean we can't compete journalistically."

Donelli groaned and rolled his eyes. "Why did I ever

believe last night might have marked the beginning of a change in our relationship?" He gave an exaggerated bow of his head. "Pardon me for insulting your professional dignity, Ms. Roberts. Now may I please have a jelly bean?"

"Just remember what happened to Chef Maurice," she warned in an ominous tone as she ungraciously plunked the jar back in front of him.

He took a handful of assorted flavors, carefully picking out the licorice ones and dumping them back in. "Don't be cute, Amanda. Actually that brings me to why I'm here."

"And here I thought you were drawn by my charm."

His lips twitched in amusement, but he left the barb unanswered. "Did you see this little item this morning?" He held out the paper, which had been turned to one of the inside pages.

"The one about Mrs. Florence Jefferson winning grand prize in the garden club competition for her roses? That's very nice for her, but I don't see the connection."

"Not that item." He jabbed his finger at the tiny headline at the bottom of the page. "This one."

Amanda sucked in her breath. "Jean-Claude is going to teach a three-day cooking course in Atlanta? Isn't returning to the scene of the crime considered bad form?"

"Where's that famous, award-winning journalistic objectivity? We don't know Jean-Claude did it. We still have to prove that."

"Are you planning to trap him next to the stove and jab him with a fork until he talks?"

"No. I thought I'd let you do that."

Her gray eyes widened. "Explain." She couldn't hide the edge of anticipation in her voice.

"I thought you should enroll in the course."

The memory of that bullet crashing through her windshield dimmed her enthusiasm ever so slightly. Its timing coincided a little too neatly with Jean-Claude's return. "Now you want my help," she grumbled.

"Well, I certainly can't enroll."

"Why not? These are liberated times we live in. Men cook. They even eat quiche."

"You can teach me how later," he said. "Will you do it? If he's a typical Frenchman, he'll probably open up better to you than he would to me."

"Flattery, Donelli? I'm stunned."

He grinned at her. "I'll have to try it more often."

"And you trust me to handle this in my own way?"

"Absolutely," he said so cheerfully that Amanda's eyes narrowed.

"How come? Not twenty-four hours ago you were still warning me to stop meddling in your investigation. Now you want me to go hang out with a man we have even more reason to believe could be the killer."

"I've had a change of heart. Besides, he's not likely to do anything in front of a roomful of people."

"May I point out that there was a whole crowd standing around when Chef Maurice keeled over."

"Just be careful what you eat."

Amanda gave an exaggerated sigh, one that she thought covered quite nicely the excitement that, despite herself, was spiraling inside her. "Okay, where do I sign up?"

Donelli gave her another little satisfied smile and she

had a feeling she'd just been had. "I knew you wouldn't be able to resist," he said smugly, getting to his feet. "I'll pick you up in a couple of hours and drive you to Atlanta. The first class is tonight. You can register at the door."

"And where will you be while I'm risking my neck?"

He grinned down at her. "In Jean-Claude's hotel room, of course."

Amanda was immediately on her feet, hands on hips. "Donelli, you rat, you're just trying to get rid of me while you do the real work."

"It did cross my mind that if you discovered the chef was in town, you might try to go after him on your own. This way there are two problems I won't have to worry about."

He took one intimidating step closer and his grin faded. Her pulse leaped. "By the way," he began, "where have you been all morning? Oscar said you were on an assignment."

She gulped, not at all fooled by his casual tone. "I was."

"What assignment?"

She drew herself up in indignation. "You sound as though you don't trust me."

"If I'm mistaken, if you were in fact at some garden party or even having your nails done, I apologize. I will buy you dinner at the elegant roadside diner of your choice." He paused to let the magnanimous offer sink in. "Shall I make reservations?"

His dark-eyed gaze never once flinched. It was Amanda who blinked.

"Well?"

She considered a flat-out lie. Then she looked into those eyes again and realized she'd never get away with it. That gaze could have made a hard-hearted felon confess.

"I stopped by Bobby Ray's."

"I don't suppose you were picking out a new dress."

"Not exactly."

"What then?"

"I wanted to see if I could get a little more information about Sarah."

He rolled his eyes heavenward. "Please, tell me you did not break into the personnel files."

"I would not be stupid enough to break into the files in the middle of the workday. If you've ever met Miss Emma Lou Timmons, you know that those records would be safe from an armed robber. By the way, where is Bobby Ray? She said he's out for the week."

"I talked to him this morning. He's following up his own leads on this case, just the way we are. He is the sheriff and, from what I hear, he's getting a lot of pressure to make an arrest. Now tell me exactly what you did this morning. I don't suppose for a minute that a visit to personnel was the only thing on your agenda."

She scowled at him. "I stopped off in the cookware department."

"Find anything you liked?"

Amanda tossed the package of glasses at him.

One brow rose as he examined them. "Lovely. Was this the extent of your morning's accomplishments?"

"No, dammit. I asked a few questions."

"And?"

She sighed in resignation. "And I found out that

Sarah had a big argument with some man before the demonstration."

"What man?"

"I was about to find that out when I got back here and ran into you."

"Amanda, you are the most exasperating woman I have ever met. Do you know something or not?"

"*I* don't exactly know anything, but I know someone who might. There's a clerk who worked with Sarah who thinks she might be able to recognize the man again. I was about to take Larry's contact sheets over for her to look at."

Donelli seemed torn between irritation and curiosity. He settled for what he obviously considered a middle ground. "Get the contact sheets. If we leave now, we can stop by the store on the way to Atlanta."

Amanda started to utter a protest, then realized the futility of it. She found the key she'd taped to the bottom of her trash can, unlocked the lap drawer in her desk, yanked it open, and reached for the prints. She found old clippings, candy wrappers and a fifteen-year-old report on the town's water supply. No prints.

"They're gone!"

"Are you sure that's the drawer you put them in?"

"Donelli, your faith in me is staggering. It's the only drawer in the desk with a lock."

"Did you lock it?"

She glared at him. "You just watched me unlock it."

"Look in the other drawers."

She went through every one of them. The prints were not there.

"Maybe Oscar or Larry borrowed them. They probably know all about the clever little hiding place you have for the key."

"I never needed a hiding place until I put the contact sheets in the drawer, and no one was around when I taped the key on the trash can."

"Let's check anyway."

She pointed Donelli in the direction of the darkroom while she began to turn the papers on Oscar's desk upside down. The only photographs to be found were those Larry had printed for the previous week's edition.

"There are no contact sheets back here," Donelli announced from the doorway to the darkroom.

Amanda sank down in her chair. "They're not out here, either."

"What about the negatives? Can Larry do another set of prints?"

"I'll call him and check, but if someone went to all the trouble of stealing the contact sheets, they probably took the negatives, too."

There was no answer at Larry's apartment. Amanda hung up the phone, a puzzled expression in her eyes. "Isn't there a Braves game on TV this afternoon?"

"Amanda, we don't have time to watch a baseball game."

"Just answer me, Donelli. Are the Braves on TV now?"

He thumbed through the paper to find the television listings. "Yep. The game started about twenty minutes ago on cable."

"Then we'd better get over to Larry's."

"You just said he wasn't at home."

"No, I said he wasn't answering the phone. If the Braves are on, he would be in front of the television. If he's not answering, then something is very, very wrong."

CHAPTER
Eight

AMANDA stuffed a new spiral notebook and a handful of jelly beans in her purse, then ran out of the newspaper office. Donelli was right behind her. The stop to grab his hat had slowed him down no more than five seconds.

"Will it offend your masculine pride if I drive?" she called over her shoulder.

"It depends on why you want to."

She turned for a quick look and thought she saw a flicker of amusement in his eyes. She dared an honest response. "I'd like to get to Larry's today."

He stopped in his tracks. "Are you suggesting for one minute that I drive too slowly?"

"Donelli, I've seen little old ladies out for a Sunday drive go faster than you do. Of course, if you'll feel threatened . . ." She allowed the comment to hang there.

"I will not feel threatened. Just to prove it, you can drive my car." He held out the keys.

She saw the trick in that. His car wouldn't move any faster than he did. "Let's take the rental I picked up thi morning. I might as well get my money's worth."

He really did look wounded now. "You don't like my car either?"

"We're wasting time, Donelli." She was torn between impatience and laughter.

"But you just insulted my car."

"I apologize. I love your car, but driving something that obviously means so much to you is just too big responsibility for me. If anything happened to it while was behind the wheel, I'd never be able to forgive my self."

He chuckled appreciatively. "Nice move, Amanda. Very diplomatic."

"Thank you. Now can we get out of here? I'm worried about Larry."

"Show me the way."

To Donelli's credit, he didn't exactly flinch when she took the first curve at fifty-eight miles an hour—maybe sixty, if she was being completely honest about it. He just pointedly tightened his seat belt.

Nor did he threaten to arrest her when the speedometer climbed past sixty-five. Instead, he murmured something that sounded suspiciously like a prayer to Saint Christopher.

Nor did he make any comment ten minutes later when she screeched to a halt in front of the small four-unit apartment house where Larry lived on the ground floor. He just reached across, removed the keys from the ignition, and tucked them in his pocket.

Amanda didn't waste time on being indignant. She

was out of the car and running up the walk before he could even work up a satisfied smirk. Donelli, apparently still not convinced of the urgency of the situation, followed at a more leisurely pace.

Halfway up the walk she heard the sound of Atlanta Braves baseball drifting through an open window. It slowed her down considerably. She suddenly felt very foolish. She also knew Donelli wasn't likely to let her forget this impulsive race across town or the laws she'd violated in the process.

She gave him a rueful smile. "I guess he must be here."

Donelli nodded. "Maybe he just doesn't answer the phone during a game."

"He answered the other day or I wouldn't have been so worried."

"And what happened the other day?"

She gave him a sheepish look. "I dragged him down to the office and he missed the rest of the game."

"A smart man would learn from that lesson."

Amanda glared at him. "Okay, Donelli. I made a mistake. But something could have been wrong," she added with a touch of defiance.

"Hey, I can't criticize you for erring on the side of caution. As long as we're here, let's check on those negatives."

Amanda preceded him into the hallway, calling out to Larry just as she lifted her hand to knock. When she touched the door, it swung open and suddenly that sick feeling she'd had on the phone returned. Her heart gave an unsteady lurch. She gazed up at Donelli in mute appeal and stepped back.

"You first, Donelli," she said in a choked whisper.

He waved her to the side of the doorway, then opened the door all the way.

"Strike three!"

The umpire's call had a particularly ominous ring to it. When Donelli pulled a gun from the holster hidden neatly and deceptively under his loose shirt, a chill raced down her spine.

"Don't move." He mouthed the words at her. She nodded. For a change, not even her stubborn, defiant streak could have budged her from this spot.

Donelli disappeared inside the apartment, leaving Amanda to quake in the stifling heat of the hallway and imagine the worst. She heard his light tread on the hardwood floors. To her nervous ears, it sounded like troops crossing a wavering wooden bridge. Then she heard him stumble. That sound was followed by a muttered oath. Her heart leapt to her throat.

"Amanda!"

Her breath came out in a whoosh of relief. It was short-lived.

"Get in here and call an ambulance." His voice was calm, but there was no mistaking the urgency.

"Oh, my God!" she said, seized by renewed and this time apparently justifiable panic. She moved blindly into the apartment and found the phone by a chair in front of the TV. She wasn't even tempted to go beyond the living room, though her eyes were repeatedly drawn in the direction of what she guessed must be the bedroom.

She recited the address to the emergency operator by rote.

"What is the injury?"

"I . . . I'm not sure."

"I need to know the injury."

"Donelli . . ." She gulped air. "Donelli, she needs to know the injury."

"Blow to the head. Possible skull fracture."

She repeated the quiet recitation, blinking back tears. Just as she hung up she heard a roar on TV and glanced up in time to see the Braves go ahead by a run on a double by the center fielder. Larry was going to be furious that he'd missed it. She sank down in the chair. "Damn. Oh, damn."

"Amanda, are you okay?"

She nodded, then realized Donelli couldn't see her. "Okay," she said in a quavering voice.

Taking a deep breath, she got to her feet and went to the doorway to the bedroom. Larry lay sprawled on the floor, blood oozing slowly from a wound on his temple. He'd apparently put up quite a struggle because the room was a mess.

Or maybe he was just a lousy housekeeper. She had no way of knowing for sure. It was the first time she'd been to the apartment, though Larry had graciously offered her a spot in front of his TV anytime she wanted it. She realized now that in his own way, he'd been trying to ease her through the divorce with a mixture of teasing flattery and friendly, undemanding companionship.

She knelt down beside him and picked up his hand, patting it in a useless gesture of comfort. He looked so young. What if he . . . ? Guilt swept through her.

"Don't start feeling guilty," Donelli said, reading her mind.

"But if . . ."

"Thinking about what might have been is useless. It happened. Be thankful you got worried and came over here. I'll never criticize your intuition again."

She blinked back more tears as she stared at Larry's ashen complexion. Donelli had grabbed the bedspread and wrapped it around him, but his skin was still cold and clammy. "Is he going to be okay?"

"Sure, bright eyes," Larry responded in a weak, thready voice. His eyes couldn't seem to focus. He blinked several times, then shut them again, defeated by the effort. "I wish it hadn't taken something like this to get you into my bedroom."

She put a hand on his cheek, noticing for the first time the light dusting of freckles. He reminded her of some tow-headed kid straight out of *Tom Sawyer*. "Oh, Larry, I'm so sorry."

"Hey, don't be. This is the most excitement I've had since I moved here." He winced. "Damn, my head hurts."

"Just stay still," Donelli advised. "We've got help on the way."

"Can't leave," Larry argued. "Can't miss the game."

"The Braves are winning," Amanda said, glad she'd caught that glimpse of the game.

"How?"

"A double by the center fielder at the bottom of the sixth."

"What happened here?" Donelli asked, obviously deciding if Larry was going to waste his breath it might as well be to give them information. Amanda knew, though, just how much he hated getting nothing more than the highlights of the game on the evening news.

"Donelli, he wants to know about the game. I'll go turn up the sound," she offered.

Larry held her back, squeezing her hand. "It's okay." He closed his eyes as another wave of pain apparently hit him. His words came out in short bursts. "Don't know . . . what happened."

"Larry, you don't have to do this now," she said, scowling at Donelli.

"Have to. Could be important. I turned on the game when I got back from an assignment." He grimaced and closed his eyes.

Finally he drew in another long breath. "Then I grabbed a beer and came in here to change my shirt." He shot her a weak grin. "I like to wear my Braves T-shirt when I watch."

"I'll bet you look like one of the team."

"What happened next?" Donelli said.

"Somebody must have been waiting for me. That's all I remember."

Amanda rocked back on her heels. "Jean-Claude," she murmured softly.

Donelli opened his mouth to ask her what she meant, but before they could get into it, the rescue squad arrived, followed ten seconds later by a red-faced, huffing and puffing Oscar. The next few minutes were spent answering the paramedics' questions and listening to Oscar grumble because no one had called him.

"What's the matter with you people?" He included Larry and Donelli in his scowl, though Amanda had a feeling it was aimed primarily at her. "You don't tell me anything. I'm not just your boss. I care about you. I get back to the office and Wiley says my photographer's dead. I almost had a heart attack right there."

"Why on earth would Wiley tell you Larry was dead?"

"Amanda, the man can't hear, remember? He must have been listening to the police radio while he was taking the classifieds on the phone. They probably said Larry had been hit on the head. The important thing is I had to hear it secondhand from Wiley, for God's sake. As if that weren't insult enough, I just found out from Bobby Ray that the windshield was shot out of your car last night."

Amanda shot a disbelieving look at Donelli. "You promised not to tell Bobby Ray."

"I didn't."

"Don't go getting your dander up, girl. The repair shop called him, which is exactly what you should have done. We can't have people getting shot up on the county roads. It's Bobby Ray's duty to see that craziness like that is stopped. He wants to talk to you later to find out exactly what happened."

Amanda rolled her eyes. "Could we save the lecture until after Larry leaves for the hospital?" She bent down to kiss his cheek. "I'll lock up when we leave, okay?"

He groaned.

"What's wrong?" she asked worriedly.

"I must be pretty bad off. I'm not even tempted to take advantage of you. Could you try that kiss again when I'm well?"

"Promise." She squeezed his hand one last time as

they lifted him into the ambulance. "Larry, do you still have those negatives from the Chef Maurice demonstration?" she asked.

"In my files. Didn't want to lose them in that chaos at the office."

"Thanks. I'll come by to see you later. Is there anyone you'd like me to call?"

"Cheryl Tiegs, but I doubt if she'd come."

As soon as the ambulance pulled away, Amanda started back inside. Oscar held her back.

"Just what do you think you're doing, Amanda?"

"I'm working a story."

"How come you're hanging around with him?" He jerked his head in the direction of the apartment, into which Donelli had disappeared.

"I am not, as you so brilliantly put it, hanging around with Donelli. Bobby Ray hired him to look into the Chef Maurice murder. I, too, am looking into that murder. It makes sense that we will occasionally turn up in the same places."

"Oh, really?" She heard the amusement in his voice and looked up to see a very knowing gleam in his eyes.

"Get off it, Oscar."

"I just don't want you to compromise that famous integrity of yours by getting too cozy with a source."

"I'll get cozy with whomever I damn well please," she grumbled and stomped back into Larry's apartment. She found Donelli already at the file. It was the only orderly thing in the apartment. Photos and negatives going back to Larry's college days were filed alphabetically, each set in its own carefully labeled folder.

"Well?" she said.

"There's no folder under Chef Maurice or murder or cooking or anything else that I can think of. Does Larry have a quirky mind? Could he have labeled it something weird?"

"From the looks of the rest of it, everything is pretty straightforward. For all of his offbeat ways, Larry is very serious about his photography. He wouldn't joke around with the files."

"I was afraid of that."

"The negatives are gone?"

"Looks that way."

"Would the two of you care to let an old man in on what the hell you're looking for?"

"The negatives from the Chef Maurice demonstration."

"Why do you need 'em?"

"We think we might have a witness who can identify someone who was fighting with Sarah Robbins the day before the demonstration. The contact sheets are missing from the office, so we came out here looking for the negatives to make new prints."

"Well, why didn't you just say so? I have the contact sheets."

Amanda and Donelli both stared at Oscar. "You do?"

"I am not the backwater newsman you think I am, Ms. Roberts." She thought his tone was unnecessarily huffy. "I knew those prints might be important. I took 'em home and put 'em in the safe."

Amanda breathed a sigh of relief. "Do we have time to pick them up now?" she asked Donelli.

"No. Oscar, keep them locked up, will you? We'll get them in the morning."

"Where the devil are you two going now?"

"Atlanta."

"Together?"

"Give it a rest, Oscar," Amanda warned.

They left him staring after them. Amanda had the distinct impression he wasn't one bit concerned about her jeopardizing her integrity with Donelli. The only thing bugging Oscar was jealousy.

Suddenly she chuckled. Donelli glanced at her curiously. "What's that all about?"

"Oscar. It's killing him not to be in the middle of this story."

"And that pleases you?"

She heard the note of implied criticism and sighed. "Not really. Maybe tomorrow I ought to tell him exactly what I have so far. He might have some ideas of his own."

She caught the quick gleam of approval in Donelli's eyes. "He might at that. By the way, what did you mean a little while ago when you mentioned Jean-Claude?"

"It makes sense, doesn't it? He knew Larry shot pictures the day of the demonstration. He even asked him about them. I'm nearly ambushed last night and then we find out he's back in town. Or back in Atlanta, which is close enough. Now this. Who else had that much opportunity and motive?"

"What about Sarah? Hadn't he already left town by the time she died?"

"I was hoping you wouldn't think of that. It's the one thing I can't explain."

"Do you still want to go to that cooking class tonight?

Maybe it would be best if you skipped it, spent some time at the hospital with Larry."

She thought about Larry, about her own damaged car. Then she thought about poor Sarah. It refueled her determination to get to the bottom of this. "You couldn't keep me away."

Donelli apparently heard the anger in her voice. He looked at her sharply. "You're only there to observe, Amanda. No subtle cross-examinations. No traps. I don't want to come looking for you and find you hanging in a cold storage locker."

"Believe me, that's not my idea of a fun way to end the evening either. I'll be careful. I'll follow directions like a true student of French cuisine."

"Amanda, you haven't followed directions since we met. I am not reassured by your sudden humble, obedient act."

She shot him the most innocent smile she could manage. That didn't seem to reassure him either.

When they arrived at the hotel, Donelli was still giving her a list of warnings. As they reached the lobby, he concluded, "And for the love of God, don't give your real name when you register."

"If I don't use my real name, exactly how am I supposed to pay for this overpriced class? I was planning on paying by check."

Donelli pulled some crumpled bills from his pocket. "Use this. I'll get it back from Bobby Ray when I turn in expenses."

Journalistically speaking, Amanda supposed that wasn't very ethical, but it was practical. At the moment, she was willing to live with practical.

With the finances settled, Donelli seemed to be waiting for her to head for the bank of elevators before creeping off to conduct his own mission. She glanced in that direction, then looked longingly toward the bar. Donelli picked right up on her indecision.

"Are you sure you want to do this?" he asked again.

"Of course I'm sure. It's a piece of cake...or *gateau*, if we're speaking French. I might as well start getting into the mood. Did I ever mention that I took French in college?"

"You're chattering."

"I'm not chattering."

"Okay, then you're delaying."

"Exactly."

Donelli chuckled. "Amanda, really, I won't think any less of you if you don't go."

She scowled at him. "I will."

This time she took two steps toward the elevators before turning back. "Just one thing."

"Yes."

"Could I have a hug?" She flushed. "You know, just in case we never get another chance to."

"We'll have other chances, Amanda," he promised. "But you can have one anyway."

He drew her into his arms and held her tightly. It was a nice hug. Reassuring. Sexy. It made her feel better.

Much better, she thought with a little sigh that bordered on a pleased purr.

When he added a gentle, lingering kiss for good measure, she felt like she could take on the world. She grinned at him.

"Thanks, Joe Donelli. You've just given me a reason to stick around for the main course."

"Glad to oblige," he said, laughing. She could tell from the look in his eyes that he meant it.

"I'll meet you back here at ten-thirty on the dot. If you're not in the lobby, I'll come looking for you, okay? So don't panic. Don't go anywhere alone. Try to stay in the meeting room until it's time to meet me. He won't try anything in there and he's not likely to want to carry you kicking and screaming through the lobby."

"Donelli, I assure you that I will do my very best not to inconvenience you or me by getting killed."

"Good, because I have some plans for later that might interest you."

That smoldering look in his eyes played havoc with her pulse. It was also reason enough to stay alive.

CHAPTER
Nine

"AH, Mademoiselle Roberts, we meet again."

Startled into unaccustomed speechlessness, Amanda looked up from the registration form to meet the dark eyes of Jean-Claude Meunier. Amusement seemed to lurk in the brooding depths. Dressed in a gray suit a shade darker than his remaining hair, he held out a hand and Amanda inserted hers instinctively, if slightly reluctantly. She watched with a sort of detached fascination as he lifted it to his lips. The fleeting, cool touch of his mouth sent a chill down her spine. She still couldn't manage to speak.

"You are Miss Roberts, are you not?" he said in a voice that might have been smoothed with honey. Though it was phrased as a question, it was said with the absolute confidence of a man only confirming a fact.

That was not the name she had dutifully written on her form, which she quickly crumpled up and jammed in her purse. Still, she saw little point now in denying her identity. Curiosity compelled her to ask, "How did you know?"

He gave her an amused half smile. "You are a beautiful woman, mademoiselle. How could one possibly forget such a face?"

The flattery gave her just the tiniest instant of pleasure before the full implication of the discovery sank in and made her palms sweat.

Jean-Claude went on as if oblivious to her nervousness, yet she knew perfectly well he was enjoying every second of it.

"You were running about after the Chef Maurice demonstration," he recalled, "asking this and that, making the notes. Then a very curious Mademoiselle Robert called my agent in New York and then me in Miami. It was not difficult to, how do you say, to put two and two together. May I ask why you are here tonight?"

Because it was his class, she supposed he could ask anything he wanted. She'd really rather he hadn't, though. She was a crummy liar, especially under pressure.

"I'm a real aficionado of French cuisine," she said. "When I saw the announcement in the paper, I couldn't resist."

"Then perhaps we shall make you the official taster tonight. You can tell the others if we have created a masterpiece."

The image of Chef Maurice smothered in cyanide-laced chocolate instantly came back to haunt her with sickening clarity. She was not at all sure she wanted to taste anything Jean-Claude had been near, much less created.

"It would be my pleasure," she lied with sheer bravado. She tried desperately to remember if she'd ever gotten around to deleting Mack from her will. She'd hate to die knowing she'd left all her worldly possessions to a two-timing louse.

"I am sure," Jean-Claude said with a devious little chuckle that would have served him well in a Bela Lugosi film.

When he had gone inside, Amanda swallowed nervously, then dug frantically in her purse until she found a soothing ice blue mint jelly bean. She had two, because they could very well be her last.

She was as brave as the next person, but this whole plan was suddenly beginning to unnerve her, especially after the disconcerting events of the last couple of days. She hadn't counted on Jean-Claude's ability to add quite so well. Damn Joe Donelli. He probably wouldn't get back here until she'd keeled right over into the bouillabaisse or whatever Jean-Claude had on the menu. Once again she considered ducking out to the nearest bar but decided she wouldn't give either of them the satisfaction.

As soon as she had paid the registration fee, she followed Jean-Claude into the meeting room and glanced around at her classmates. There were only a handful, mostly women, and yet Jean-Claude treated them as graciously as he might have an overflow crowd.

As the class progressed, Amanda found that she was relaxing. In fact, she was enjoying it. Her fear began to abate as she basked in that Gallic charm she had first experienced on the pages of his cookbook back in Sarah's kitchen. Though Jean-Claude was far from handsome, his demeanor made him attractive, even sexy, in an understated way, sort of like the French singer Charles Aznavour. Jean-Claude was also blessed with a subtle wit and an irreverent flair that was one part Julia Child and one part Galloping Gourmet.

His jacket had been tossed aside during the introduction. He rolled up his shirtsleeves and loosened his red tie. Ingredients and instructions flew with haphazard abandon. Pens raced across notebooks as the students tried to keep up. Amanda gave up midway through the recipe and sat back to enjoy the show. Laughter and generous servings of a fruity, full-bodied French wine warmed the atmosphere. Pens finally lay idle.

A plump chicken was dangled by one leg, examined critically, then plunked unceremoniously on the counter. When it slid to the floor, Jean-Claude shrugged dramatically and picked it up.

"*Pauvre poulet,*" he murmured sympathetically as he gave it a comforting pat. He doused the chicken liberally with wine, then took a sip himself—from the bottle. Amanda wasn't sure if the chicken's dousing was for flavor or antiseptic purposes. In Jean-Claude's case she was sure it was for the sheer enjoyment of it.

It was all the act of a consummate showman, far more entertaining than Chef Maurice. Amanda found herself thinking it was a terrible shame that the younger chef's sexy looks had catapulted him to undeserved fame, leaving the aging Jean-Claude on the short end of the audience competition. Even the demonstration at Bobby

Ray's store in the middle of nowhere had drawn a larger crowd to see Jean-Claude's successor.

It was especially sad because the last two hours had convinced her that Jean-Claude was truly a Frenchman with a genius for cooking, and Chef Maurice seemed more and more like the fake Jean-Claude had called him.

Increasingly she found herself hoping that he'd not been the one to kill the chef, but facts were facts. He'd had the opportunity and the motive, and though he'd clearly guessed that she suspected him, Jean-Claude had said nothing to defend himself.

"What was he supposed to say?" she chided herself mentally. *"Just to set your mind at ease, Mademoiselle, it was not I who laced Chef Maurice's soufflé with poison"?* It was more dramatic than hello as a greeting, but a little unlikely. Perhaps his refusal to defend himself made an even stronger statement about his innocence.

Damn. This entire evening—with the help of the wine—was making her head spin.

She forced herself to try to think the whole thing through logically. She examined each of the possibilities, jotting the names down in her notebook: Jean-Claude; Jonathan Webster; perhaps Sarah, if you believed the murder-suicide theory; the most recent addition, Tina Whitehead. There were a couple of longshots: the missing brother and the mysterious man that Sue Ellen had overheard arguing with Sarah. Realistically, Jean-Claude still belonged at the top of the list.

An enthusiastic round of applause interrupted her musings. Jean-Claude was flushed with pleasure.

"*Merci*, my friends. Thank you. We will see you tomorrow for lesson two. Until then, *adieu*."

His gaze caught Amanda's. "Mademoiselle, could you stay for a moment? We have things to talk about, do we not?"

Nothing that couldn't wait until Donelli and his gun showed up, Amanda thought, though she nodded. She peeked at her watch. It was already ten-thirty. Could Donelli be far away?

When the others had gone, Jean-Claude found two wineglasses and poured them each a drink. "I will drink first, *ma cherie*," he said dryly. He sipped slowly, savoring the wine.

Amanda squirmed uncomfortably. Guilt at his having guessed her suspicions and fears made her take an especially long, repentant swallow of the delightful wine.

"So, mademoiselle, why are you really here tonight? Do you hope, as your American detectives say, to pin the rap on me?"

Amanda wasn't quite sure how to answer that. She could say no and watch him hoot his disbelief. Or she could tell him the truth and wait to see if she joined the list of victims. She wasn't wild about either alternative.

"I didn't do it, you know," he said, taking the choice out of her hands. It was exactly what she'd hoped to hear him say, but it didn't ring quite as true as she would have liked.

"Chef Maurice was once a student of mine," he went on. "I considered him a friend."

"But he stabbed you in the back."

"A colorful turn of phrase under the circumstances and not quite accurate, since he is the one who is dead."

"You know what I mean."

"Yes. Of course I do. I apologize for the levity. It is just that you seem to take this jealousy between us so seriously when I do not. It is the way of life. Wasn't it your Andy Warhol who once said, 'The day will come when everyone will be famous for fifteen minutes'? I had my fifteen minutes and they were glorious."

"But you can't have been happy about what happened."

"Not for the reasons you think, *ma cherie*. I know I am the better cook, the more ingenious creator. I do not need fame in America to tell me that. In France I am still highly regarded. I feel bad, though, that someone I once knew well would choose to appear as a fake, as something he was not, when such a charade was so unnecessary."

"I don't understand. Are you saying he was jealous of your continued success in France? Wasn't it only a matter of time until he succeeded there as well?"

"*Non, ma petite.* Chef Maurice would never have been acclaimed in France. He might have understood the cuisine, but he did not speak the language as a native. He would have been found out at once as a fraud. The French would not have forgiven him that."

Amanda's eyes widened. "He wasn't French?"

"No more than I am American, just because I speak the language with some skill and am able to make a hamburger."

"Tell me about him, then. Anything you remember about his real background. Tell me who you think might have been responsible for his death."

Jean-Claude sighed and closed his eyes wearily.

Amanda waited. She glanced up just in time to see Donelli walking past the door of the meeting room. She tried to catch his eye, tried to signal to him that all was well, but he seemed to be into his role as undercover passerby. She wasn't sure how long he expected to get away with it before Jean-Claude noticed that he was pacing in front of the door with the timely precision of a guard at Buckingham Palace.

She concentrated very hard on getting an ESP message through his thick skill. She was convinced that at any moment Jean-Claude was going to turn his denial into a confession or, at the very least, give her enough background information to solve this entire mystery.

Donelli, unfortunately, did not seem to have her patience. Nor was he responsive to ESP. The sound of silence must have been some sort of warning call to his well-trained ears because the next thing she knew he was storming into the room like the point man on a SWAT team.

Jean-Claude's eyes snapped open and his defensive mask dropped firmly back into place.

"Who are you?" he demanded, his eyes narrowing.

"Joe Donelli." His smile was disarming. Even Amanda was impressed. For a man who'd come into the room intent on mayhem, he'd switched gears with astonishing ease. He was apparently more intuitive than she'd guessed. She'd have to compliment him about that later. "I'm here to pick up my friend."

He cleverly avoided the use of any name because they hadn't settled on her pseudonym earlier. He turned his smile on her. "How was the class?"

The question seemed idle enough, but it was the lift

of Donelli's dark brows that hinted to Amanda that she was expected to give him some sort of a signal.

"It was terrific," she said, giving Jean-Claude a beaming and well-deserved smile. "There's some left-over quiche if you'd like to try it. You won't believe the crust. And the coq au vin was *magnifique!* Too bad you didn't get here sooner."

Donelli seemed disappointed that there was no need for a dramatic rescue. "Are you ready to leave?" he said grumpily.

"Jean-Claude and I were just getting acquainted," she said pointedly. "Perhaps we could all have a drink in the bar."

"Perhaps your young man is impatient to be alone with you," Jean-Claude said, seeming almost relieved at the reprieve. "I don't blame him. You're a lovely young woman. Perhaps we can talk more after class tomorrow."

"Certainly," Amanda said. "I'd like that."

"I will walk with you to the lobby then."

The three of them chatted idly during the elevator ride, then crossed the lobby together. Suddenly the hotel doors opened with a flourish and a woman swept in. With her tousled auburn hair, the dramatic clothes, sparkling expensive jewelry, and an astonishing amount of luggage, she drew stares from everyone. Jean-Claude, however, did more than stare. He muttered an expressive French curse under his breath.

Amanda stared at him. "You know her?"

"*Mais, oui.* It is the lady barracuda. She is the one responsible for what happened to Maurice, you can be sure of that. The blame is all at her feet."

Donelli and Amanda exchanged stunned glances.

"Who . . ." Donelli began.

"Tina Whitehead." Jean-Claude turned unexpectedly and took Amanda's hand, bowing over it gallantly. "Until tomorrow, *ma cherie*. I must leave you now. Suddenly I feel quite ill."

He looked it as well, his complexion suddenly pale, his eyes after an initial flare of anger turning lifeless.

"What do you suppose that was all about?" Amanda said when she and Donelli were alone.

"He doesn't seem to approve of the Lady Tina."

"Do you think there's anything to what he said? Could she have been responsible for the chef's death? She was in New York when it happened."

"We don't know that."

"Shouldn't you go and talk to her?"

"Not tonight. I want to get some idea what brought her down here first. My guess is she'll be on Bobby Ray's doorstep first thing in the morning demanding that Chef Maurice's body be released to her."

"Either that or she'll be calling for an immediate arrest of the most likely suspect. She looks like the type not to wait around for the wheels of justice to turn."

They watched until Tina Whitehead had checked into a penthouse suite and disappeared into the elevator. Once the show was over, it didn't take long for Donelli to forget Tina and get back to telling Amanda exactly what he thought of the way he'd found her cozying up earlier to their prime suspect.

"Good Lord, Amanda, you were supposed to be getting information, not getting into bed with the guy," he said as they began the ride home. Donelli, she noticed, had gotten behind the wheel of her rental car without so much as glancing at her for permission.

"You sound jealous." She tried carefully to guard against any hint of delight creeping into her voice.

He glowered at her. "That's unfortunate. I meant to sound furious. What the hell did you think you were doing?"

"Trying to get some answers," she retorted huffily. "And I would have gotten some new information, too, if you hadn't barged in there. He was just telling me that he's known Chef Maurice since the very beginning, that he was no more a Frenchman than you are. He even dropped a few hints that we're looking in all the wrong places for the killer."

"By that, I assume he's figured out that he's a suspect."

"If he didn't know it before, I'm sure he figured it out when my bodyguard showed up."

"Okay. It's my fault. I'm sorry as hell for worrying about you. Maybe you'll have better luck tomorrow. I'll wait in the car until I see the ambulance arrive."

"I don't know what you're getting so huffy about. You're the one who sent me into the lion's den."

"Obviously another lapse of judgment on my part. I thought you had sense enough to tread carefully."

She lifted one delicate brow disdainfully. "Perhaps we should change the subject. Did you find anything strange in Jean-Claude's room?"

"I wasn't crazy about his underwear."

"Donelli!"

He sighed. "No. I didn't find anything that would connect him with Maurice's death."

"I'm not so sure he did it."

"I thought he was your prime suspect."

"He was until I got to know him. Now I just think he's lonely and a little sad. I don't think he's a homicidal maniac."

"Amanda, I'm a little worried about these gut-level reactions of yours. You empathized with Sarah, so that ruled her out. Now you feel a little sympathy for Jean-Claude, so he must be okay. If you keep meeting the suspects and deciding what fine folks they all are, it's going to be mighty difficult to make an arrest."

"You promised to trust my intuition."

"Prematurely, it seems."

"Well, you certainly don't want to arrest the wrong person, do you?"

"Let me pose a hypothetical question. If all of the evidence points to someone you instinctively like, what do you expect me to do?"

"Convince me that the evidence is overwhelming. Think of me as sort of an advance jury."

"And in the case of Jean-Claude, this jury is leaning toward acquittal?"

"I still have an open mind."

"How reassuring."

She patted his hand. "Don't worry, Donelli. I have the utmost faith in you. I'm sure you'll find the real killer."

"I appreciate your confidence."

The remark lacked sincerity, but his fingers curled around hers and Jean-Claude's guilt or innocence suddenly seemed less and less important. It registered in some distant part of her mind that the car had stopped.

"Amanda . . ." His voice was thick and trailed off uncertainly. An emotion that had nothing to do with his earlier impatience flared in his eyes and she recalled the promise he'd made to her before he'd sent her off to that session with Jean-Claude.

Just as the muscles deep inside her tightened in anticipation, she realized they were parked in front of the newspaper office rather than her house.

"Why are we here?"

"So I can get my car."

"But you said . . . you implied . . ." She glared at him. "Never mind."

"I promised that we'd have some time together later," he replied softly.

"Okay, yes. That's exactly what you said. What are you, Donelli, some sort of tease?" she snapped, furious with herself for allowing it to matter. For heaven's sake, she had practically forgotten all about it herself, so it couldn't be that important to her either. Still, there was an empty place inside her that she filled with outrage.

He reached across and ran a finger along the curve of her clenched jaw. "Ah, Amanda, I'm sorry if I gave you the wrong idea."

"Don't be sorry," she grumbled. "Just explain."

"I got to thinking while I was checking things out at Jean-Claude's."

"It's flattering to know I was on your mind when you were trying to catch a murderer."

His lips curved into a rueful grin. "I find you come to mind a lot more than I'd like."

"You'll have to pardon me if I'm having a little trouble keeping up with your logic here. You can't get me out of your mind, so you're letting me go home alone. Is that it?"

Suddenly he chuckled. "Who said I was sending you home alone?"

Her eyes narrowed. "But . . ."

"What I was thinking was that we both ought to have our cars in the morning because I have to meet Bobby Ray very early."

"Oh."

"Indeed."

Irritation rose, then fled, replaced by relief and something more, something better, something incredibly exciting. To cover the confusing range of her response, she grumbled, "Just get your car, Donelli."

"And do you still want me to follow you home?"

"Do whatever you like."

He searched her eyes, then nodded in apparent satisfaction. "I'll see you in a few minutes, Amanda."

She shrugged indifferently, but her heart leapt to her throat. All the way home, she was aware of Donelli's headlights shining in her rearview mirror. Her nerves fairly hummed with anticipation. Only once did she have second thoughts, but before she could dwell on them she had parked her car and Donelli's was beside it. Then he was opening the door and drawing her out and into his arms. In his embrace she found she couldn't think at all.

"There's still time to change your mind," he whispered as his lips found a tender spot near her ear.

"No," she said softly. "It's much too late for that."

"Do I hear a note of regret in your voice?"

Her lips curved in a faint smile at his perceptiveness. "It's nothing you need to worry about."

"It's just that you hadn't planned on getting this involved with anyone in Georgia."

The remark struck home as he'd known it would. "Well, you know what they say about the best-laid plans."

Then, before he could start worrying about the implications or the future or regrets, she stood on tiptoe and touched her mouth to his. She sought the velvet and fire that would carry them beyond hesitation, that would turn the sweet ache of longing into urgent demand.

She found what she was looking for in that tentative, inquisitive kiss and in the breath-stealing one they shared just inside the front door and in the explosive one that came as he carried her into the bedroom. For a seemingly straightforward, uncomplicated man, Donelli was amazingly expert in the nuances of a kiss, capable of gentle subtlety and fiery possession. By the time his hands swept away her clothing and glided over burning flesh, Amanda was aware of nothing except the need to know more of him.

She explored flat planes and taut muscles, hair-roughened expanses and satin-sheathed hardness. With uncertain fingers and loving lips she caressed and teased and tasted until Donelli's body was as familiar to her as her own.

When she was trembling with desire, when his need matched her own, still he held back, gazing into her eyes, asking questions she was not prepared to answer.

"Just love me, Donelli," she pleaded. "I need to feel you inside me, filling me up, taking me with you."

He brushed the hair away from her damp brow and, eyes never leaving hers, entered her slowly, that first stroke an exquisite torture, followed by a sure, hard thrust. It was a rhythm that tormented and delighted, but one destined to accelerate into a more urgent pace. It was the look in Donelli's eyes that shattered her and set off a wild burst of some long-forgotten emotion even before her body rocked with an explosion of feeling.

It was only when her pulse had slowed again and the ecstasy had faded that she met Donelli's gaze again. His arms were still around her, the length of his body hard against hers. But in his eyes she saw surprise and something she recognized as fear. She knew that's what it was because it reflected her own tumultuous feelings so closely. *This*—she refused to put a name to it—was not supposed to be happening to her. To them.

But it had.

CHAPTER

Ten

DONELLI was gone when Amanda awoke. She rolled into the still-warm empty space where he'd slept and hugged his pillow to her. The masculine scent of him surrounded her, a scent of musk and spice and perspiration that was definitely erotic. A sharp reminder of how easily he affected her senses, it was also faintly disturbing and she didn't have time for lingering over the feelings that had swept through her so unexpectedly the previous night. She decided it was just as well he'd gone or she'd never have gotten to all the things she had planned for her day.

She was going to swing by the hospital to visit with Larry, then stop by the office, pick up the contact sheets Oscar had kept hidden at home and take them straight to Sue Ellen. Sue Ellen would identify the man she thought had fought with Sarah. Amanda would have an essential clue and then she would...what? Go to Donelli with the information? Tell Bobby Ray? Traipse off for a confrontation of her own just to be sure she wasn't falsely accusing someone? The latter would be a little tricky with Donelli watching her every move. And, as she knew very well by now, it could be dangerous.

Still, she thought, it wouldn't be fair to just take Sue Ellen's word for what had happened at the department store, would it? Every journalism professor she'd ever had had insisted on the need for verification. The rule of thumb had been two sources on every report, especially if it was controversial and there was any room for doubt about the accuracy.

Thus convinced that it would be her duty to carry the investigation to its logical conclusion before turning the evidence over to the authorities, she set off for the hospital. There she found Larry grumbling at the nurses and tugging at the too-short hospital gown.

"You seem to be better."

"I want to get out of here."

"What does the doctor say?"

"Umm. I see. Umm," he mimicked. "He apparently has a limited vocabulary."

"I see."

He scowled fiercely. "Don't you start. I suppose you're still working that murder story. Did you find out anything about who'd clobbered me in the head and stolen the negatives?"

"Not yet, but it turns out Oscar has the contact sheets. I'm on my way now to pick them up and show them to someone who might be able to help." A thought popped into her head. "Larry, are you sure the person who hit you didn't say anything? Could he have had an accent?"

"You mean like Southern? Or maybe French?"

"Whatever."

"Sorry. If he said anything at all, I've forgotten it."

"Could you tell if he was tall or short?"

"I didn't see him."

"I know, but maybe by the way he grabbed you."

Larry's brow furrowed in a frown, then his eyes lit up. "You know, I think he must have been tall, at least as tall as I am. Unless the guy was tall or standing on a chair, he couldn't have hit me quite so hard or from the angle he did."

Amanda's mood brightened. Another clue in Jean-Claude's favor. He was barely as tall as she was and didn't appear especially strong. Tina, on the other hand, was fairly tall for a woman and seemingly robust. "Thanks, Larry. Is there anything I can bring you?"

"You might try hiding a file inside a cake."

"I think that's for jail escapes."

He cast a significant glance around the room. "Well."

Amanda brushed a kiss across his forehead. "Rest, hardhead. I'll talk to you later."

From the hospital, she drove straight to the office. For the first time since she'd taken the job, she could hardly wait to get there.

Then Oscar took the proverbial wind right out of her sails.

"I want you to get over to Miss Martha Wellington's this morning," he said the minute she walked in the door. "She just called. She says it's important."

Dumbfounded, Amanda just stared at him. "Oscar, we're right in the middle of this murder investigation. I can't waste an entire morning making small talk with Miss Martha."

"And her friends."

"Her friends?"

"It's a meeting."

"I don't care if she calls it a nuclear summit, send someone else. I'm busy."

"Amanda," Oscar said, in his patient, long-suffering tone, "in case you haven't noticed, this paper is not overrun with general assignment reporters. You're all I've got. I can't put out a weekly with one story in it just because it's all you feel like doing. We're a community newspaper. Folks expect us to tell 'em what's been going on in the community."

"I don't suppose you want me to comment on that," she said. She was so exasperated she threw three jelly beans in her mouth without even checking to see what flavors they were.

"It's not necessary. You've made your feelings known about the dearth of excitement in these parts. Now are you going to get on over to Miss Martha's or aren't you?"

Amanda knew it wasn't really a question. She sighed. "Okay, Oscar. What's the occasion?"

"She's having a tea to talk about the preservation of the Milstead place as a historic landmark."

"Isn't the Milstead place that tumbledown eyesore on the road to Lawrenceville?"

"That's the one."

"Why on earth would anyone want to preserve it?"

"It's old. Somebody famous probably slept there. I don't know. You'll have to ask Miss Martha."

It had been Amanda's experience that asking Miss Martha Wellington anything about her beloved Gwinnett

County was like opening a Pandora's box of musty linen. She had first encountered Miss Martha under less than idyllic circumstances. Mack had discovered the popular local historian soon after their arrival. The two of them had spent hours chatting happily about the most obscure details of local history while Amanda was left to drink Miss Martha's weak English breakfast tea with its thin wafer of lemon floating on the top.

Miss Martha lived in a lovely old brick house with pale green shutters. Her backyard was heavily wooded. Beds of azaleas filled the front lawn with color in the spring. Amanda had always been able to comfort herself with the reminder that if it was necessary to be bored, at least she was doing it in a gloriously tranquil setting.

This morning there were already several cars in the sweeping circular driveway. Amanda could hear the excited hum of conversation from the screened-in porch at the side of the house. The front door stood open, displaying the wide hallway that ran the full length of the house to an open door at the back. The hardwood floors gleamed. An Oriental vase filled with yellow roses in full bloom sat on a small antique stand. The scent drifted past on the breeze.

Even though the door was open, Amanda rang the bell and waited for the tap of Miss Martha's cane. As near as Amanda could tell that cane with its intricately carved handle was mostly for show. Miss Martha moved with a sprightly gait for someone well into her eighties.

"Well, now, Amanda. How delightful to see you again. You come right on in here," she said. She turned with a regal flourish and tap-tapped her way back to the porch with Amanda trailing along behind. "We've been waiting for you, haven't we, girls?"

Half a dozen lively, elderly faces peered at Amanda and nodded. She hadn't seen so many hats, flowered silk dresses, and white gloves in years. Lavender and lily of the valley cologne competed, luring Amanda into a riot of memories of similar gatherings at her own grandmother's house on Long Island.

"Why don't you sit right over here, dear?" Miss Martha said, picking out a footstool beside her own rattan chair. Amanda immediately felt she'd been relegated to court recorder for the queen.

Miss Martha then began her ardent defense of the Milstead home. It was clear that the speech was primarily for Amanda's benefit. The small cabin with its peeling paint, sagging roof, and yardful of tangled, waist-high weeds suddenly came to life again as Miss Martha talked, her blue eyes snapping with excitement. Built in the early 1800s by one of the first white pioneers to come to this part of the state, the house deserved to be on the National Register, she said staunchly.

"This is our history. If the future is to mean anything, we must look to the past. If progress destroys our heritage, how will our children learn of their forebears? How will they see firsthand what life was like for those early settlers who braved a land that until then had been inhabited only by the Creeks and Cherokees? The Milstead house may not be as famous or as important as Judge Elisha Winn's, but that doesn't mean we should let it fall to ruin."

Breathless, her papery cheeks flushed, she sat back

amid enthusiastic applause. She looked at Amanda. "Did you get all of that, dear?"

"Yes, ma'am. How do you propose to finance the restoration? Do you intend to ask for public funds?"

Miss Martha looked aghast at the very idea. "Why, no indeed. We will raise the money, just as we have in the past. We will hold bake sales and solicit private donations. We will hold tours of other historic homes. We can do it, can't we, ladies?"

"Yes, Miss Martha."

"Oh, my, yes."

There was a veritable chorus of approval. Amanda hadn't a doubt in the world that these ladies could do whatever they set their minds to.

"Then we're all in agreement?" Miss Martha asked.

Heads bobbed enthusiastically. There was no need for a vote. The conclusion had been foregone before the meeting ever took place. But Miss Martha was no fool. She knew she needed the support of these public-spirited ladies if she was to get the job done. She tactfully included them in the decision making.

"Now, then, shall we have tea?" Miss Martha suggested, picking up a small silver bell from the table beside her and ringing it imperiously. "I believe Della has baked a lovely coffee cake as well."

Amanda stood to leave. "I'm terribly sorry, Miss Martha, but I can't stay. I'm working on another story and I have to get back to it."

"That murder, I'm sure," she said in a hushed voice.

"Yes."

"What a distasteful business. I'm surprised at Oscar for subjecting you to it, my dear. It has everyone quite upset. I was talking to Bobby Ray about it after church just last Sunday and telling him he should make an arrest soon before all of us are too afraid to leave our homes."

"I'm sure there's nothing for you to worry about, Miss Martha," Amanda reassured her. "I don't think the murder had anything to do with anyone around here."

"Why, of course it did. That lovely Sarah Robbins was practically one of us. We all knew her. Why, Bobby Ray even brought her here for tea once so we could all get to know her better."

Amanda had forgotten for a moment what small towns were like. "I'm sorry. I wasn't thinking."

"Don't apologize, dear. Just be careful. We'd hate for anything to happen to such a lovely new addition to our community."

Amanda made a speedy escape after that and drove back to the office, proud of herself for not once exceeding the speed limit. It would have pleased Donelli.

It took her exactly twenty-seven minutes to write a short report of Miss Martha's plans for the Milstead place. She handed it to Oscar. "Now, where are the pictures?"

"You're like a puppy dog nagging at a bone, you know that?"

"It's not a bad trait for a reporter, Oscar."

"I suppose not." He handed her the contact sheets. "Now you be real careful with these things, girl. Until Larry gets out of the hospital, we can't get copies made. These are all we've got."

"I'll guard them with my life," she promised, then winced and hoped like crazy it wouldn't come to that.

"By the way, Joe Donelli called while you were at Miss Martha's. He wants you to call him before you go see this sales clerk. He says he'll meet you there."

"Okay." She headed for the door.

"Aren't you going to call him?"

"I'll call him from the store."

"I don't think that's what he had in mind. How about I call him for you?"

"I'll call him myself, Oscar. I promise."

And she would, she thought as she drove to the Johnson and Watkins Superstore. She'd call Donelli just as soon as she'd had a little time alone with Sue Ellen and the contact sheets.

At the store, she took the steps of the escalator two at a time. Once she reached the cookware department, she searched high and low for some sign of Sue Ellen. The girl wasn't anywhere on the entire third floor. Finally Amanda approached a woman in the linen department who was folding a stack of blankets. They were red, just like the one that had been used to cover Chef Maurice. A shudder swept through her at the memory.

"May I help you?" the woman asked cheerfully.

"I'm looking for Sue Ellen. Is she working today?"

"Yes, indeed, but she's gone to lunch. I can help you, if there's something you need from cookware."

"No, I must speak with Sue Ellen. It's a personal matter. Did she go out to lunch?"

"No, I don't believe so. She usually brings hers from home. You might take a peek in the staff lounge. It's right across the floor, behind the sporting goods. You can't miss it. Bobby Ray seemed to have some crazy idea we'd enjoy the lounge more if we could look out and see the fishing rods and basketballs. Guess he thought it would be the next best thing to being able to get out and use them."

"Thanks."

Amanda circled the third floor and walked through sporting goods, wondering if she ought to pick up a can of tennis balls as long as she was here. After she saw Sue Ellen, perhaps. She walked through the archway to the lounge, then stopped in her tracks.

Donelli looked up from half a tuna fish sandwich and smiled.

"I wondered when you'd get here."

"Did Oscar call you?" she asked suspiciously.

"No and neither did you, from what I gather."

"I was going to."

"Of course you were." He pulled out the chair next to him. "Sit down and join us. Sue Ellen says she always brings enough for an extra person. You can share my sandwich."

Amanda ignored Donelli's outstretched hand with the tuna fish sandwich in it and faced Sue Ellen with a smile. "How are you?"

"Just fine, Miss Roberts. Did you bring those pictures you wanted me to look at?"

"I have them right here. Would you like to finish your lunch first?"

"No need." She patted her stomach. "Jimmy Joe says I've already gained more weight than I did with the first baby and this one's not due for another two months. Besides, I've only got a few more minutes on my break."

Amanda drew the contact sheets out of their envelope

and spread them on the table in front of Sue Ellen. "Just take your time. We want you to be sure it's the right man."

Amanda sat on the edge of her chair and watched Sue Ellen study the pictures. The girl tugged thoughtfully on a strand of hair as she looked, shaking her head as she dismissed one picture after another. Donelli was sitting back and enjoying the whole thing, his hat perched on the back of his head as he calmly munched on the sandwich and took the last of the potato chips from Sue Ellen's bag. Every time he crunched down on one of the chips, Amanda's nerves snapped. She glared at him. He gave her one of his most beguiling—and infuriating—smiles.

"Here he is," Sue Ellen said at last. "Right here." She was pointing at exposure number seventeen on the fifth roll of film that Larry had shot.

Donelli looked at the picture, then at Amanda. Her heart seemed to sink straight down to her toes.

"It can't be Jean-Claude," she protested weakly.

Sue Ellen apparently heard the regret in her voice. "I'm sorry. Did I do something wrong?"

"Not at all," Donelli reassured her. "You've been a big help."

"Of course you have," Amanda said, trying to inject a note of gratitude into her voice. The important thing was to solve the case, wasn't it? Not just to prove her own theories were correct?

She gathered up the contact sheets, put them back in the envelope, and stood up. Donelli rose in the leisurely way of a man with no place important to go. She was surprised he didn't stretch and yawn.

"I don't suppose I need to ask where we're going next," she said.

"We?"

"If you're going after Jean-Claude, I'm damn well coming with you. Besides, I have my class with him tonight." Just to make her point, she started out the door of the lounge.

"I'm not so sure they won't have to get along without the instructor."

She stopped where she was and stared at Donelli. "You can't arrest him."

"I can't?"

"I mean, doesn't Bobby Ray have to do that?"

"I'm sure that can be arranged." That smug smile was back. He passed her in the doorway. "If you're coming with me, Amanda, let's go."

She drew herself up to her full height and inquired nastily, "Are you aware that you have a particularly unpleasant touch of arrogance when you're right?"

The insult didn't seem to reach its mark. "So you've said." His grin widened.

Still grumbling under her breath, Amanda followed him from the store, but when she started across the parking lot to her car Donelli took her elbow. "Uh-uh. We're going in my car this time."

She saw no point in arguing. Besides, Bobby Ray was probably paying for his gas. Oscar never gave her a cent for hers.

The car bounced over the road like a mobile steambath. Amanda tried to ignore the uncomfortable heat by thinking of Alaska in midwinter. Then she thought of

Donelli and his smug smile buried under an avalanche of snow. It had a reasonably soothing effect.

Donelli apparently took her silence for sulking and set out to cheer her up by pointing out the historic sights along the way.

"I have spent the entire morning with Miss Martha and her friends. I don't need another lecture from you, thank you very much."

"I just thought, in light of what happened between us last night, that maybe I should start trying to persuade you that Georgia does have a few things to offer," he said in mild reproach.

"I know that. I am fond of the peaches. And Atlanta is reasonably civilized."

"A stirring tribute."

"It's the best I can do at the moment."

"You aren't going to sulk forever because you made a mistake about the murderer, are you?"

"I am not sulking and I don't know that I've made a mistake. For one thing, he's not tall enough."

"I beg your pardon. Is there some rule about all murderers being a certain height?"

"Only this one." She explained her conversation with Larry."

"I suppose you think it was a casual burglar with a fetish for negatives."

He ignored her sarcasm. "Come on, Amanda, how much irrefutable evidence is it going to take before you admit that Jean-Claude did it?"

"A confession would be nice."

Donelli scowled at her. "I'll see what I can do."

A confession, however, was not forthcoming from

Jean-Claude. Amanda quietly applauded his Gallic indignation at Donelli's cautiously worded accusations.

"Mr. Donelli, let us talk facts, not suppositions, shall we?" Jean-Claude said.

"By all means. Did you go to see Sarah Robbins before the Chef Maurice demonstration?"

"No."

Donelli persisted. "Think back, Mr. Meunier. Are you sure?"

"Let us approach this from another angle. At what time and on what day was I supposed to have been there?"

"Saturday. Early afternoon. About two-thirty, I believe."

"No. I was right here in Atlanta all afternoon. I was making a chocolate mousse in full view of hundreds of chocolate lovers. I believe there are any number of people who can confirm it. In fact, you might even be able to see some television footage that would back up my claim."

That rocked Donelli back on his heels. Amanda silently cheered.

"But you did go to the store on the day of the demonstration?"

"I did."

"Why?"

"I wanted to see Maurice. I wanted to try to convince him not to continue with this insane charade of his. Sarah persuaded me to leave."

"Sarah?" Donelli pounced on Jean-Claude's use of her first name as eagerly as he might have on a full confession. "You knew her?"

"But, of course. She was using her real name—Sandra Reynolds—then. She and Maurice were together when he first came to me for instruction."

"Sue Ellen said you seemed to be arguing."

"I would not call it that. As I said, she felt I shouldn't be there. She felt the day would be stressful enough because of . . ."

"Because of what?"

"Because his brother was coming."

As bombshells went, Jean-Claude had just detonated a dandy.

CHAPTER

Eleven

"HIS brother?" Donelli and Amanda said in a chorus. They exchanged startled looks. By silent agreement, Donelli turned the questioning over to Amanda. That surprised her, too. And pleased her.

"What was his brother doing there, Jean-Claude?"

"I do not know precisely, though I suspect it had something to do with the suit he had filed against Maurice. A very messy business, I understand. You could ask Mademoiselle Whitehead. She was quite familiar with the details. In fact, I believe she had been named in the suit."

"Did you see the brother at the demonstration?"

"We have never met. I would not have recognized him."

"But Sarah told you he was expected?"

"Indeed. He had appeared in her office threatening to disrupt the demonstration. That is, perhaps, the argument to which Mr. Donelli was referring earlier. She said it was a very frustrating conversation. Nothing she said could calm him or convince him to stay away. She was anticipating the worst. Though I never knew her well, her agitation was apparent even to me. In retrospect, it seems she was quite correct to be frightened."

Amanda tried very hard not to gloat when she suggested to Donelli that perhaps they were interviewing the wrong suspect. "Maybe we should give Miss Whitehead a call now and see what she can add to this."

"May I go now to prepare for my class?" Jean-Claude asked.

"Of course," Donelli said. "Thank you for your time. You will remain in town for a few days, won't you? Just in case we need to speak with you again."

"I will stay as long as my schedule permits, Mr. Donelli," he said, then added with a slight smile, "unless you find sufficient cause to hold me here."

Donelli took the deliberate taunt well. When the two men shook hands it was as if a new understanding had been born between them.

Then Jean-Claude turned to Amanda and took her hand, lifting it to his lips. This time she thoroughly enjoyed the gallant gesture, to say nothing of the irritated gleam it put in Donelli's eyes.

"I assume I should not expect you tonight, Mademoiselle Roberts?" Jean-Claude said with a touch of his dry humor. "You have found a more enticing menu, perhaps?"

"I'm sorry. Would you save me the recipes?"

"But, of course."

And then he was gone, his pace brisk and confident. It was definitely not the demeanor of a guilty man.

Amanda was three steps ahead of Donelli in the race to the house phones. She decided he probably wasn't trying very hard. Maybe it was his way of conceding the victory for this round to her.

The phone rang twenty-two times in Tina Whitehead's room before Amanda gave up. "No answer," she told Donelli.

"Then I'll buy you a drink and we'll try again later."

In the dark little bar off the lobby, Donelli ordered a beer. Of course, she thought. A man like Donelli would always drink beer. Amanda asked for a glass of white wine.

When the waitress had gone, an odd tension began to build inside her. She guessed Donelli felt it, too. He was absentmindedly tearing one of the cocktail napkins to shreds. When the drinks finally came after a seemingly endless wait, she took the first sip before finally saying what was on her mind.

"This is really weird, Donelli."

A knowing half smile played about his lips. "What is?"

"This. You and me actually sitting down together, having a drink. It's like a date. We'd never done anything quite like this before, well, you know, before last night."

"Uh-uh," he said adamantly, going to work on another cocktail napkin. "It's not a date."

Surprise and the first hint of apprehension nagged at her. "You say that like dating is a dirty word."

"Maybe for you and me it is."

Amanda's heart sank. "Second thoughts, Donelli?"

He sighed heavily. "Something like that. It has occurred to me, in the bright light of day, that I could get to like you very much."

She ignored the tremor that swept through her at that announcement because she had a feeling something far less positive was yet to come. "So?" she asked cautiously.

"You're very determined to leave Georgia and I am not a masochist. I think before things go any further with us, we both need to do some clearheaded thinking."

"Don't you suppose we could date while we think?"

"No way. I've already told you my feelings about you and me dating. It's too dangerous. I can't think straight with you in my arms."

"Neither can I," she admitted quietly. "But I don't want to stop."

He peered at her. "I'm not saying we won't see each other."

"Then we will date."

"Dammit, Amanda, I would feel a whole lot better if you stopped talking about this dating stuff. It's been my experience that you can talk a relationship to death."

"Is that what happened to your marriage?"

"No. My being a cop is what happened to that."

"She hated it?"

"She liked the idea of it, the image. She thought it was sexy. In fact, I think it was the main reason she married me, that and the fact that it infuriated her parents. As it turned out, she hated the reality of being a cop's wife."

"I think I might have liked you as a cop, Donelli."

He looked straight at her then, surprised. "Yeah?"

She nodded.

"Maybe it's too bad we didn't meet sooner, then."

"Maybe so."

A silence fell between them and to Amanda it seemed burdened with regret. She couldn't face the silence or the regrets.

"Talk to me, Donelli. We need to start communicating better."

"What are you talking about? We communicate, don't we?"

"About the case, if you can call that communicating. Mostly we fight. We don't talk about much else. I certainly don't feel like I really know you."

"Why would you want to? I mean you're going to go hotfooting it out of town the minute one of those papers gives you a call."

"That doesn't mean we couldn't be friends."

"I've got friends, Amanda."

Suddenly she was overcome by an odd sense of loss. "You don't need another one? I thought everybody could always use another friend."

"I need more than that, especially from you," he said softly. There was no missing the desire behind the words. She swallowed hard and tried to avoid his gaze, but now that she'd started this discussion, he was having none of her evasive tactics. He held her chin and looked right square into her eyes until she could feel the heat from that look all the way down to her toes.

Why the devil did it have to be a man like Donelli who made her feel that way? He irritated her. He was perfectly content in his retirement to farming, though she still wanted to be in the middle of the action, tilting at windmills. Even when they shared something, like this case, they butted heads constantly.

"Seems to me you need more than a friend, too, Amanda," he was saying now in that low, gentle voice of his. It caressed and brought her senses alive. She wanted to be back in bed with him deep inside her. "Don't you need somebody to keep you warm at night? Somebody to keep you out of trouble or maybe bail you out of it, if you get into it anyway? Somebody who won't go through the roof when you get all involved in some story and forget to fix dinner? Don't you want somebody you can tell whatever's on your mind and know that you won't be judged, just loved?"

His fingers stroked her cheek and now Amanda couldn't have looked away if she'd wanted to. Warmth flooded through her, exactly the kind of good feelings Donelli had been talking about. She felt right about this moment, even for some reason about this uncomplicated, straightforward man.

But not about this place. She could not stay in this place, even for him. "Donelli, tell me what to do," she said wistfully.

His sudden chuckle diffused the tension. "Amanda, you haven't taken my advice about anything yet. Why would you want to start now?"

"Because I'm confused. Sometimes—not always, mind you, but sometimes—I like the way you make me feel. God knows I did last night. A part of me wants more from this relationship, but dammit you're right. If that call comes from a paper up North, I'll go. And I'll hate it if that hurts you."

Donelli picked up his beer and took a long drink, watching her as he did. He set the glass down carefully. "Then, as I see it, what we have here is definitely not a date. It's a business meeting."

Amanda raised her hand to touch his cheek, but he caught it in midair, gave it a squeeze, and put it back on the table. "It's okay, Amanda. If this is meant to be, we'll work it out. I'm a patient man."

It was, she thought, another one of the things that drove her crazy. "I'm not patient, Donelli."

"So I've noticed." There was a rueful note in his voice. "Don't worry about this, Amanda. The timing's just not right yet. Why don't we give Tina another call?"

His calm, accepting attitude irked her. "Forget Tina. Forget the damn case for two minutes. I want to talk about you and me, Donelli."

He shook his head. "Right now, there is no you and me. Talk's not going to make the difference. Now are you going to call Tina or shall I?"

"You want to talk to her now, you call," she snapped, hoping he'd get away from the table before the ridiculous, inexplicable tears she felt brimming in her eyes spilled down her cheeks.

While Donelli was gone, she tried recounting all of his bad points. She focused especially hard on his occasionally superior attitude, his mule-headed stubbornness, and his desire to prevent her from doing her job when he thought it might be dangerous.

"It wouldn't work," she muttered finally, satisfied

that those wistful yearnings she'd felt earlier had been only a temporary aberration. Her overwhelming responsiveness in his arms was probably nothing more than the result of too many lonely months since Mack had left her.

When Donelli still hadn't returned fifteen minutes later, she added rudeness to his list of sins. After another five minutes, she paid the check and went looking for him. It would be just like him to have gone venturing off on his own to conduct this interview. If he had, it was entirely possible that Bobby Ray would have another murder to investigate.

Funny how Bobby Ray had just popped into her mind, she thought, looking across the lobby and spotting him. He was sitting on a deep-cushioned mauve sofa with the glamorous Tina Whitehead beside him. She looked perfectly at home, as though she were entertaining a delightful guest in her own living room. Donelli was nowhere to be found.

Amanda debated the appropriate tactics for the situation. Bobby Ray's presence dictated that it might be best not to go rushing in with some unfounded accusations. In fact, it might be very wise if she sort of slipped up on the two of them unnoticed. She might be able to learn a thing or two before making her presence known.

She chose her path through the lobby with great care. Several large potted palms behind the sofa provided the perfect cover for what she had in mind. She tiptoed into the middle of the plants.

"I do understand your position, Miss Whitehead, but much as I'd like to get this whole thing resolved, I can't possibly make an arrest yet," Bobby Ray said. "I have an investigator working on the case and as soon as he feels there is sufficient evidence, I assure you Chef Maurice's murderer will be taken into custody."

"I am telling you it is that awful man, Jean-Claude. If you had only heard the things he said to me this morning, you would know he is the killer."

Amanda's dislike for the woman grew as her rantings about Jean-Claude went on. "Methinks the lady doth protest too much," she muttered under her breath.

"Is that so?" a familiar voice whispered right back.

Amanda whirled around so quickly, it was amazing she didn't take a palm tree or two with her. "What is the matter with you?" she hissed into Donelli's amused face. She dragged him out of earshot of Bobby Ray and Tina. "Were you trying to scare me to death or did you merely want to blow my cover?"

"You call that a cover? If you're going to barge into these things, you need to work on your technique."

"Do you have a better approach?"

He seemed to ponder the question. "Now here's an original thought: Why don't we just join them? Or is that too straightforward for you?"

Amanda glared at him. "Whatever you like, Donelli."

It was just as well that they'd made that decision because Bobby Ray had caught sight of them.

"Why, here's my investigator now, Miss Whitehead. Joe, why don't you and Miss Roberts come on around here and tell us the latest."

Tina Whitehead surveyed Amanda thoroughly from beneath amazingly thick, dark lashes and then dismissed her. Her gaze lingered more appreciatively on Donelli. She patted the spot next to her on the sofa and purred invitingly, "Yes, Mr. Donelli, do join us. Bobby Ray has been telling me how terribly good you are."

The suggestive tone in her voice had to be a mistake, Amanda thought grumpily. Bobby Ray certainly wouldn't be telling Tina how good Donelli was at *that*.

She had to admire Donelli's handling of the situation. He deftly seated Amanda in the place beside Tina and sat down in a chair beside Bobby Ray. That brought a dangerous glitter into Tina's eyes that Amanda decided suggested murderous intent. She moved Tina to the top of her list of suspects. Donelli, however, must have been taken in. He was smiling at her.

"Miss Whitehead here was just telling me how anxious she is to have this case resolved," Bobby Ray drawled. Amanda took a good look at him for the first time and noticed how haggard he looked. It appeared the pressure of this case was getting to him, but at least he wasn't rushing into making an arrest.

"You finding anything, son?" he asked Donelli.

"I think we may have something in a few days, perhaps sooner," Donelli said. "Miss Whitehead, you could help. Would you mind giving me a little background information about Chef Maurice? I understand he was not only your client, but a close friend."

"That's true. We met about five years ago in New York, through a mutual acquaintance. He was studying French cooking at the time."

"With Jean-Claude Meunier?"

"That's correct."

"Was he planning to do cookbooks even then?"

"No, he merely wanted to be a chef in a fine restaurant. I persuaded him that he had much more potential than that. We began to create a plan for making him a celebrity."

"Did you know a Sarah Robbins back then?"

Amanda was impressed by the blank look Tina directed at Donelli. "No, I don't believe I ever heard the name."

"What about Sandra Reynolds?"

A spot of high color dotted her cheeks, but she met Donelli's gaze directly. "I believe we were introduced."

"Was she involved with Chef Maurice at that time?"

"I believe so."

"Is it fair to say that you replaced her in his affections?"

Her eyes narrowed. "Mr. Donelli, exactly where are you heading with this line of questions? My relationship with Maurice was hardly a crime. We were consenting adults. If that little nobody got hurt, it's her own fault. She would have held him back."

Amanda had to fight to control her fury on Sarah's behalf. Even Bobby Ray looked indignant.

"Where were you on the day she was killed?" Amanda asked coolly.

Tina seemed to freeze at the blunt question and her expression hardened. Donelli grew very still. If he was irritated by her directness, he kept it to himself.

Amanda had met a lot of women like Tina Whitehead in New York, women who took what they wanted without regard for anyone else. As long as they were in control, things went smoothly. They radiated charm. When challenged, they displayed their claws.

"Well?" she persisted.

Tina met her gaze with a challenging stare. "I don't believe I have to answer to you."

"Then try it for me," Donelli suggested. "Where were you?"

"I was in New York."

"I suppose you can prove that."

"If necessary."

Bobby Ray looked thoroughly befuddled by the sudden animosity and the hard-hitting questioning. "I'm sure that won't be necessary, Miss Whitehead," he said apologetically. "Joe here's not really suggesting that you had anything to do with those deaths, are you, Joe?"

Donelli caught Amanda's eye for just an instant, warning her to let it go for now. Then he turned one of those high-powered, lazy smiles on Tina. "Not for the moment. You could tell me one or two more things, though, if you don't mind."

Tina visibly relaxed. Her own smile returned. "Why, of course, Mr. Donelli. I want to do everything I can to help."

"Tell me about this suit that Chef Maurice's brother had filed."

She looked startled. "How do you know about that?" Then she shrugged. "Never mind. I can guess. Jean-Claude couldn't wait to fill your ears with more of his nonsense, I'm sure. The man's jealousy is notorious. I'm surprised you haven't found the evidence you need to arrest him already."

"Perhaps we will yet," Donelli said. "In the meantime, I'd like to know a little about the suit."

"Such a silly thing," she said with a dismissive wave of her bejeweled hand. "Maurice's brother is a grasping little man. He couldn't bear it that Maurice had won so much acclaim."

"What exactly are the charges of the suit?"

"I'm not sure of the legal details. You'd have to ask my attorney," she said and Amanda sensed immediately that she was lying. A woman like Tina would know every comma in a suit that threatened her income.

"Then you were involved as well?" Donelli said.

"Yes," she admitted with great reluctance.

"When was the suit to go to court?"

"You'd have to ask my attorney."

Amanda had watched Tina closely throughout Donelli's questioning and guessed that this suit was more of an irritant than she was admitting. From what Jean-Claude had told her, she guessed that Chef Maurice was likely to be exposed as a fraud with Tina named as a coconspirator. She wondered what Tina's reaction would be to that.

"I'm curious," she began innocently. "Was Chef Maurice truly a Frenchman?"

Tina's eyes sparked angrily. Too angrily, perhaps. It gave her away even before she spoke. "Why on earth would you ask a question like that? Of course, he was French."

"I don't know. There was something about his accent that troubled me. Besides, it does strike me as odd that a Frenchman would come to New York to study French cooking when the most famous culinary schools in the world are right in France. I thought perhaps that was something that might come out if the suit went to trial."

Tina apparently decided it was pointless to go on with

the bluff. "Okay. You are right. He was not French. And it would have come out if that brother of his had his way, but so what? It would have done no real harm. Now it would be pointless to reveal it and malign the reputation of a dead man."

"I think that's enough for now," Donelli said suddenly. "Amanda, you and I should be going."

"But . . ."

"Now," he said, drawing her to her feet. "Thank you again for your cooperation, Miss Whitehead. I'm sure Bobby Ray will keep you informed about any progress on the case."

"I'll be talking to you real soon, boy," Bobby Ray said. "Why don't you plan on meeting with me down at the sheriff's office first thing in the morning?"

Donelli nodded his agreement as he propelled Amanda through the lobby.

"What's the hurry?" she demanded. "All of a sudden you've decided that there's something that can't wait?"

"I want to get back to the newspaper office."

"Why on earth would you want to do that?"

"I gave Oscar a call earlier and asked him to make some calls to the wire services to see what he could find out about this suit. He was going to see if there was a photo on file of the brother."

"That's where you were when you ditched me in the bar with the check?"

"I didn't ditch you, Amanda. I came back. You're the one who got impatient again."

She held out her hand. Donelli stared at it. "What's that for?"

"I want four-fifty."

"I beg your pardon."

"That's three-fifty for the drinks and I left a dollar tip."

He pulled out his wallet and extracted a five-dollar bill. "I thought you were a liberated woman."

"I am. You're not a liberated man. I don't want you to feel guilty for sticking me with the check."

He chuckled and put the five dollars back in his wallet. "I think I can live with the guilt."

"Donelli!"

"You want to pay for the parking, too?"

"Go to hell, Donelli."

Once they were finally settled in the car—Donelli paid for the parking—they went over everything Tina Whitehead had told them.

"I think she did it," Amanda said.

Donelli rolled his eyes. "I suppose I should be thankful that there's finally a suspect you don't like."

"I'm serious, Donelli. We haven't checked out her alibi. She could have been down here the whole time."

"We'll trace her movements, Amanda, but why would she kill off her lover and his ex-lover?"

"Maybe she found out that Maurice was going back to Sarah after all. Tina did not strike me as a woman who'd take rejection well."

"You were just envious of all those diamonds she was wearing."

"I was not envious. Even you have to admit they were a little overdone, though. Three rings, a necklace, and earrings so big they could be pawned to finance a major motion picture."

"She's the type of woman who can carry them off."

"She reminds me of an expensive call girl. If it had been winter, she'd have been draped in mink."

"I don't think her jewels or her taste in winter coats are on trial here."

"You don't think expensive taste can provide a motive for murder? Let me try this scenario on you. She finds out that her biggest client, who just also happens to be her lover, is about to dump her, personally and professionally. She stands to lose a fortune."

"So she kills him? I don't buy it. She still loses."

"Not if she's holding a huge insurance policy on him."

Donelli laughed. "You don't know there's any insurance policy."

"You don't know there isn't one," she said stubbornly.

"Okay, Amanda, we'll check that, too." He pulled up in front of the newspaper office. "Now let's go see what Oscar has."

Oscar had three wire stories on the suit, including one just three days before the murder indicating that it was to go to trial at the end of July. The wire service had also sent a picture of the brother. Amanda took one look at it and her eyes widened.

"It can't be."

"It can't be what?" Donelli demanded.

"Let me get my notes from the demonstration." She

found the notebook in her desk drawer and began flipping through the pages. "Here it is, right here."

"Here what is?"

"I interviewed that man at the scene, not more than ten minutes after Chef Maurice died. He told me he'd never heard of the chef, that he was just there to buy an electric can opener for his wife. He also said his name was Henry Wentworth."

CHAPTER
Twelve

I T was one of the few times Amanda had felt she had both Oscar's and Donelli's undivided attention. It was a heady feeling. She described the brief encounter with the man who'd called himself Henry Wentworth.

"He seemed a little nervous and distracted, but everyone was in such a state by then that I didn't give it much thought. Did you interview him, Donelli?"

"No. He must have gotten away before I got there. I'm sure he was on the next flight back to New York or wherever."

"Maybe not," Amanda said thoughtfully. "Let's not forget about Sarah. She knew he was coming. She was afraid something terrible was going to happen and it did. If Henry or whatever his name is murdered Maurice, he'd know that Sarah was likely to give him away. He couldn't afford to let her talk."

"But it was over a week later when her body was

found. Do you think he would have stayed around that long before killing her?" Donelli asked. "I can't see it."

"It doesn't make sense to me, either," Oscar agreed. "He'd have knocked her off right away and then been on that plane out of here."

Amanda had to concede they both had a point.

"Do those stories say where he lives?" Amanda asked.

Oscar scanned them. "No street address, but he must live in New York if that's where the suit is filed."

"I guess that means I'd better get up there," Donelli said. He picked up the phone and began to dial.

"Who are you calling?" Amanda asked.

"Bobby Ray. I want to tell him what we've learned and make sure this trip is what he wants."

A minute later, he said, "Hey, Bobby Ray, this is Joe. I'm glad you're back from Atlanta. I've got some news."

He outlined what they'd discovered, that the chef's brother had been at the scene of the murder and, based on what they knew from Tina and Jean-Claude, had a motive for killing Chef Maurice. "I was thinking of taking a run up to New York to see if we can wrap this up."

Amanda watched as Donelli's jaw tightened. "Yeah, I know the kind of pressure you've been under," he said. "But you can't go around making arrests just because some state officials or the victim's girlfriend want the case closed. Tell Ms. Whitehead to cool her jets or maybe you ought to question her about why she's in such a rush. Does she have something to gain by putting an end to this?"

Amanda grinned approvingly. She still thought the venomous Tina was a very likely suspect herself.

"Okay. Okay," he said with a touch of impatience. "I'll call the minute I know anything. Don't let anyone leave town and that includes Jonathan Webster and Ms. Whitehead."

As soon as Donelli had Bobby Ray's approval, Amanda looked at Oscar hopefully. Oscar looked at Donelli. "You really think you can crack this case while you're up there?"

"It certainly looks like the break we've been waiting for. At least this brother should be able to fill in the missing blanks."

Oscar nodded. "Okay, Amanda, pack your bags."

To her surprise there wasn't even a hint of reservation in his voice. She started to throw her arms around him, but noticing his startled expression she settled instead for a quick kiss on the cheek. "Thank you."

"Just don't go staying in one of them fancy Central Park hotels. We don't have an unlimited expense account around here." He scowled at Donelli. "And try to tie up all the loose ends in a hurry, will you? We can still get it in this Thursday's edition."

"We'll do our best to meet the deadline, Oscar," Donelli said solemnly, though Amanda had the distinct impression he was trying not to chuckle at Oscar's priorities.

As she and Donelli hurried out the door, she glanced back and saw Oscar sit down heavily at his desk. For the first time since she'd known him, he looked tired and defeated. She sensed instinctively what was wrong. It was the biggest story ever to hit these parts and he was feeling left out. She remembered the way he'd been acting the other day at Larry's and felt guilty for not doing something about it sooner.

"Wait for me a minute, will you, Donelli?"

"Amanda, we've got to get moving."

"I won't be long."

She went back in and sat on the corner of Oscar's desk. One of his expressive eyebrows shot up disapprovingly and she got back to her feet.

"I was just thinking. Do you think maybe you ought to handle this from now on, Oscar? You are the editor after all. Folks expect you to do the big stories. You could go to New York with Donelli and I could stay and take care of things around here."

He met her serious gaze with a pleased expression. Suddenly she was very glad she'd made the offer. Oscar shook his head, though.

"It's your story, Amanda, and you're doing a hell of a job. I'm not going to take over now. That's not the way the business works."

"Are you sure?"

"I'm sure," he said. "But thanks for asking. Now get out of here. Donelli's looking impatient."

That, Amanda thought with a certain amount of glee, had to be a first. "I'll call you from New York and let you know how it's going. You might think of some leads we ought to check out."

Things moved at a breakneck pace after that, just the speed she liked. They stopped by her place and Donelli phoned for plane reservations while she packed a carry-on bag. Then they stopped for his things. By eight o'clock they were in the air and Amanda was struck again by that same sense of nervous anticipation that had bemused her in the hotel bar in Atlanta. She was going to New York, her favorite city in the world, and she was going with Donelli. It stirred a tempest of disturbing thoughts.

How would it feel going back after all this time? How would it feel to know she had to leave again after experiencing that excitement and energy for a few days? Was there any chance at all that Donelli would discover he had missed all the things New York had to offer?

The minute the flight landed in New York, Amanda headed straight for a pay phone.

"Can't wait to call all your friends, huh?" Though the taunt was spoken lightly enough, she suspected the emotions underlying it went much deeper.

"I'm not going to call my friends. I'm going to look up a phone number for Henry Wentworth."

Donelli's best smile came back; the one that made her heart lurch. "You're looking in the W's. I doubt if it's listed under his phony name."

Amanda let the heavy directory fall back into place. "Wiseass."

"Even the best of us make mistakes, Amanda. Try Rosen. That's the name on the suit. Henry Rosen."

"I knew that."

"Of course you did."

There were several listings for a Henry Rosen. "Should we just start calling?"

"Amanda, it's already after ten. By the time we get checked into a hotel, it'll be eleven. It can wait until morning. He doesn't know we're after him. He's not likely to go anywhere."

"I don't want to wait until morning. What if he's gone to work or something?"

"Then we'll find him at work or we'll wait until he gets home."

She regarded him impatiently. "Donelli, what exactly was your arrest record in Brooklyn?"

"Very good. So was my conviction rate, just in case that was your next question. How about yours?" he inquired cheerfully. "Any credits besides the Yankovich case?"

"Okay. You've made your point. But I hope you're prepared to stay up all night talking to me because I won't be able to sleep a wink until we get this guy."

"An interesting idea," he said in a provocatively low tone. "I'll give it some thought."

That sense of standing on the edge of a precipice returned and made her palms sweat. Her remark had been entirely innocent. She had not meant to go planting any dangerous ideas in Donelli's head. She'd decided he was probably right about the importance of keeping things cool between them. This feeling in the pit of her stomach right now was anything but cool.

She avoided Donelli's gaze, swallowed nervously, picked up her suitcase, and headed for the taxi stand. She decided it would be very smart to keep her mouth shut until she figured out how to keep her foot out of it.

At the midtown hotel he'd picked, Donelli checked them into separate rooms. They weren't even adjoining. Still, the look in the desk clerk's eye suggested he didn't believe for a minute that both of those rooms would be used. Amanda suspected they would be. Again she reminded herself it was probably just as well.

The bellman took them to her room first. Donelli waited in the doorway. He was looking very edgy, as if standing on the threshold of her hotel room might be a little more temptation than he'd planned to deal with. The bellman pointed out the air-conditioning control, the light switches, the room service menu . . . He probably would have gone on, but Amanda interrupted him by handing him a tip. He took the hint. Donelli looked relieved. The instant the bellman left, Donelli waved good night and disappeared down the hall behind him.

"Well, what the . . ." Amanda began indignantly, staring after him. For all her rational arguments against it, she'd been hoping for a kiss at least. She shut the door very, very quietly, then picked up a pillow and hurled it at the door. She was reaching for another one when someone knocked. It was Donelli. He still looked uncomfortable.

"Maybe we should talk for a while."

"In here?" she asked skeptically.

He looked at her, looked at the bed and the one chair, and shook his head. "Downstairs in the bar."

Amanda picked up her purse and went with him. When they were seated at a table and their orders were taken, she said, "This is getting to be a habit, Donelli. Are all of our most intimate conversations going to take place in a bar?"

"Who said anything about an intimate conversation? I thought maybe we could talk about tomorrow."

"Tomorrow?" she repeated blankly.

"Yes," he said very firmly, then looked around, a scowl on his face. "Where the hell are those drinks?"

"Patience, Donelli. They're coming now."

It apparently wasn't the drink he wanted so much as the napkin. Within seconds he'd ripped it to shreds. It was getting to be a predictable sight. Amanda sipped her wine and waited for him to explain what they were doing there because he obviously had his own agenda and it had nothing to do with relieving their pent-up hormones.

"Can any of those friends you've got up here get you a look at the court documents?" he asked finally.

"No problem. They're public record. I can go to the courthouse myself in the morning."

He nodded, clearly happier to be on familiar, impersonal turf. "Okay, while you do that I'm going to get some of my friends out in Brooklyn to run a check on this guy to see if he's been in any trouble before."

"Other than a correct home address and the basics of the suit, is there anything in particular you want me to look for in the record?"

"Just be sure you clarify Tina Whitehead's role in all this. I don't like the way she's pushing Bobby Ray. If there's time, you might check around and see if there's any information on an insurance policy."

Amanda nodded, then smiled at him. "Thank you."

He stared at her, clearly mystified. "For what?"

"For not treating me as though I'm just in your way up here."

"Why would I do that? I've never said you weren't a good reporter, Amanda, just an impulsive one. As long as you don't decide to go after Henry Rosen on your own, I'll have no complaints."

She shuddered. "I think you can count on me to wait for you for that. I still haven't forgotten about those shots that were fired at me or about what happened to Larry."

"Okay, then, I guess that's it. Let's get to bed."

Amanda couldn't contain a grin. "It's nice to see your direct style carries over to everything, Donelli. I might have hoped for something a little smoother, but what the heck."

"Very funny, Amanda."

He did kiss her good night, however, at her door, but chastely, on the cheek. Dammit.

Only after she'd closed her door and had time to think about it did she decide that Donelli had been very wise. A continuation of their affair would only complicate things. They had work to do in the morning. They had lives to lead when this was done. Separate lives.

Or did they? That one night in Donelli's arms had told her a lot about the state of her own emotions where he was concerned. A part of her wanted to explore the possibilities. Another part feared they were moving onto dangerous turf. It was that part that was grateful to Donelli for keeping his distance. The other part couldn't get to sleep.

When she finally did doze off, she was plunged into the midst of some very erotic dreams. When she awoke, she felt energized. She gave the credit to New York, then admitted it might have a little something to do with Donelli.

As soon as she'd eaten the bagel and cream cheese she'd ordered from room service, she got on the phone to Tina Whitehead's office.

When the receptionist answered, she asked for Miss Whitehead's secretary.

"Yes, this is Debra. May I help you?"

"I hope so, Debra. I would like to make an appointment with Miss Whitehead to discuss your firm's insurance needs."

"Insurance needs?"

"Why, yes," she said in a deliberately perky sales pitch voice. "You have so many successful clients, I'm sure you must insure them against the unlikely event that they would become incapacitated and no longer able to perform. We have a program which I believe is the best around."

"I'm terribly sorry," Debra apologized. "Miss Whitehead has dealt with the same firm for years. She's been very satisfied with the coverage. I don't believe she has any desire to change."

Amanda allowed herself a brief moment to enjoy her triumph, then said, "I can certainly understand that. Just for my records, so that I can explain to my boss why I didn't have a meeting with Miss Whitehead, would you mind giving me the name of the firm you already deal with?"

Debra mentioned a major insurance underwriter.

"Thank you very much for your time."

Bingo, Amanda thought as she began flipping through the phone book for the firm's number.

Once she was connected with the right department, it took only a few carefully worded questions and the hint that Miss Whitehead was thinking of increasing the size of the policy to determine that Tina already carried a million-dollar life insurance policy on Chef Maurice.

"Score one for my side," she muttered as she picked up her purse and headed for the courthouse. She left a note at the desk for Donelli giving him the news and saying she'd meet him at noon at one of her favorite restaurants on the West Side.

The court documents painted a particularly sordid picture of Chef Maurice's integrity, to say nothing of his lack of brotherly love. Henry Rosen had charged that his brother—Morris Rosen—had stolen recipes from him and then conspired with Tina Whitehead to use them for self-promotion while shutting him out of the profits. He requested damages in the amount of $1.6 million or one-half of the chef's earnings at the time of the trial. Because Tina and Chef Maurice had formed a corporation, she was named as being equally liable.

"That's a mighty expensive soufflé," Amanda murmured. "I wonder what happens to the suit now?"

She found a pay phone and made a call to a very bright, very ambitious lawyer she had worked with on the Yankovich story. "Tom, it's Amanda. Do you have a minute?"

"For you, doll face? As long as you want. Are you here in the city?"

"For a couple of days. I'm working a story."

"Tell me what you need."

"What would happen if a suit was filed against two people, but one of them died before it could be brought into court?"

"It could be brought against the estate of the dead person as well as against the remaining defendant."

"So it wouldn't just be dropped?"

"Not unless the plaintiff wanted to call it off. Are you going to tell me what this is all about?"

SHERRYL WOODS

"Not right now. I have some more pieces to fit into the puzzle."

"Let me know when the picture's finished, okay? You've got me curious."

"You're always curious. You're the one who should have been a reporter."

"It helps when you're a lawyer, too."

"You've been an angel. Talk to you soon."

"Wait. Are you still living in the hinterlands?"

"Don't say it like that. It's not so bad," she heard herself saying. She wasn't sure if she was defending Georgia because she was beginning to like it or if she was just plain defensive about still being there. At any rate, she suggested, "Come on down and visit. You'll find there is civilization outside of Manhattan."

"Sweetheart, I'm entrenched here. It's not in my best interests to make a discovery like that. Take care, love. Stay in touch."

Amanda left the courthouse and caught a taxi. "Lincoln Center, please," she told the driver and then settled back for the slow crawl through midday traffic. She used the time to try and analyze the information she'd found. Would it make sense for Henry Rosen to kill his brother when the suit was about to go to trial? And what about Tina? Wouldn't it have made more sense for her to kill Henry than to have poisoned Chef Maurice?

She played through several scenarios once she and Donelli had been served with thick pastrami sandwiches in a deli across the street from Lincoln Center.

"I'm still betting on the brother," Donelli said. "Like your lawyer friend told you, he can still go on with the suit. He doesn't lose a thing, except a brother he'd grown to resent."

"But Tina stands to gain all that insurance money."

"She may have to give a big chunk of it to Henry."

"She'd probably still have some left and don't forget she was probably furious when she found out Maurice was cheating on her."

"There's no point in speculating about this all afternoon. Let's go see Henry."

They found his apartment a few blocks away in an area that was beginning to be restored. His particular building hadn't seen a coat of paint in the hallways in years and the linoleum on the floor was cracked and peeling. The original color was no longer even discernible. Although the other names on the mailboxes were barely legible on curled, yellowing paper, Henry Rosen's was neatly typed on spotless white paper. It seemed a tiny rebellion on his part against the overall dinginess.

They climbed the stairs to the third floor and knocked. "Yes, who is it?" a faint voice called through the door.

"Joe Donelli, Mr. Rosen. I'm investigating your brother's death."

"You have some identification?"

"A driver's license. That's it. I'm working unofficially."

The door opened a crack, but the chain remained in place. "Let's see it."

Donelli passed through the license. Henry Rosen nodded at last, then caught sight of Amanda. Though the lighting was too dim to tell for certain, he seemed to go quite pale.

"Hello," she said quietly. "I believe we met in Georgia. You told me then that your name was Henry Wentworth. I'm Amanda Roberts."

The door closed and there was the rattle of a chain before it opened again. "I suppose you might as well come in."

Looking at Henry Rosen more closely now, Amanda noticed that there was a slight resemblance between him and Maurice. Henry was clearly older and smaller. He also appeared weary, but there was a spark in his blue eyes that seemed familiar. She recalled something Jonathan Webster had said much earlier about just that. Without even realizing it he had noticed Henry in the crowd that day and recognized something familiar in him, at least on a subliminal level.

"May I bring you some coffee?" Henry asked politely.

"I could use a cup," Donelli said. Amanda suspected he wanted to give the man time to collect himself. He'd clearly been taken aback by their appearance on his doorstep.

Henry joined them several minutes later with a tray laden with cups of fresh-brewed coffee and a plate of homemade cookies. The plate and cups were chipped, but the attempt at graciousness was superb. Amanda felt an instant's trace of pity for this man who had been left to walk in his brother's shadow.

She also wondered exactly how safe it was to eat the cookies.

"Mr. Rosen, tell us about your relationship with your brother," Donelli said.

Sudden tears welled up in the man's eyes and he dabbed at them impatiently with a pristine white handkerchief. "Despite what you must think, I loved my brother. We were very close until that horrible woman . . ."

"Tina Whitehead?"

"Yes. Until she came into the picture and began filling Morris's head with grandiose ideas. We had made so many plans, you see. I was already working in a restaurant, developing a following of sorts. We were going to open our own restaurant as soon as Morris finished training. Every night we would talk about our dream, Morris, Sandra, and I. We could have had tremendous success with my recipes, Morris's charm, and Sandra's skills. She was going to help us with the decorating. As you may know, she is a woman of superb taste."

Amanda caught his use of the present tense and darted a quick look at Donelli. He had obviously noticed it, too.

"Mr. Rosen, this Sandra you mentioned, you are referring to the woman who called herself Sarah Robbins when she moved to Georgia?"

"Yes. I'm sorry. I had forgotten that is how you would know her."

"Are you aware that she is dead?"

The blunt question had the effect of a stunning blow. Henry Rosen's eyes widened and his mouth dropped open, then twisted. He looked like a man in agony.

"No," he said softly as he wrestled with the harsh truth. "It can't be."

His astonishment and pain seemed genuine. "I'm sorry," Amanda said. "You knew her very well?"

"Almost as well as Morris did, perhaps better in some ways. Sandra and I could always talk. She was devastated when Morris left her for that Whitehead bitch. I tried to convince her to stay here, to try to win him back. In the end I'm certain she would have won, but she refused. She had too much pride. She wanted to forget all about Morris. She thought she could start over again in someplace completely new. She refused even to keep in touch. I had no idea where she'd gone until I saw her at that store in Georgia."

"Did you argue before your brother's demonstration?"

"Yes. I had flown down there to try one last time to reason with him before the trial. I thought we could settle things between us without the ugliness of a court fight. Sandra tried to talk me out of it. She said she would talk to him, but I was adamant. We exchanged angry words, I'm sorry to say. I told her it was something I had to do myself. I don't know exactly what I was going to say to him the next day. I suppose one part of me wanted to cry out during that demonstration, to make a scene, but that was not my style. I decided to wait and see him afterwards."

"And is that what you did?" Amanda asked.

"Yes. I was downstairs in the store, waiting near the front door for him to leave, when I began to hear the rumor that something had happened. I rushed to the third floor. That's when I ran into you, Miss Roberts."

"You had not been on the third floor earlier that day?" Donelli asked.

"Absolutely not."

"You appeared very calm when I met you," Amanda said. "Why did you give me a false name?"

"I was in shock. I knew, because of the suit, I would be under suspicion. It was an instinctive gesture. I needed time to gather my wits."

"Because you were guilty?" Donelli pressed.

"No!" he said adamantly. Then his voice shook with emotion. "I did love my brother, Mr. Donelli. Despite everything, I wanted a reconciliation. He was the only family I had."

"Mr. Rosen, do you own a gun?"

Henry Rosen's eyes widened. "A gun? Of course not. Why would you ask? That isn't . . . dear God, that isn't how Sarah was killed, is it?"

"No. But there was an incident, involving Miss Roberts, in fact. Someone shot at the windshield of her car, apparently in an attempt to keep her from reporting on this story."

"I assure you it wasn't me. I've never even held a gun. They terrify me."

"All right," Donelli said. "Let's talk about something else for a moment. On the day prior to the demonstration, did you see the ingredients for the demonstration while you were with Miss Robbins? Sorry, while you were with Sandra?"

"No. That's one of the reasons she was so impatient with me, I think. She was trying to rush out to buy them when I saw her. She was so afraid everything wouldn't go smoothly. Just like always, she was willing to do anything for my brother, despite all the heartache he'd caused her."

"Did you go with her to make the purchases?" Amanda asked, earning an approving nod from Donelli.

"No. I left then and went back to my motel room."

"Did you see anyone who could confirm the time you arrived there?"

"Yes. I asked the desk clerk about places to eat dinner. I'm sure he could confirm the time. It must have been about four o'clock."

"After your dinner, did you remain in your room until the next day when you left for the store?"

"I went to the motel coffee shop for breakfast, but other than that I was in the room until eleven o'clock, when I left to drive to Johnson and Watkins. The maid might be able to confirm that. She stopped several times to ask if I was ready for her to clean the room."

"After your brother's death, did you come back here immediately?"

"No. I stayed in Atlanta for several days. I thought Sandra might need me. We tried to offer each other some small measure of comfort. Mostly we talked about the past."

Amanda thought of the disarray in Sarah's kitchen and wondered if Henry had been her mysterious visitor. "When was the last time you saw her?"

"On the Wednesday night after the demonstration. I had to fly back. I was expected at my job on Saturday. I swear to you, she was alive when I left, though she was still deeply troubled."

"Because of your brother's death?"

"That, of course," he said. He looked directly at Amanda. "But I also believe she knew who killed him."

Amanda's eyes blinked wide with surprise, though his remark was not entirely unbelievable. She, too, had wondered how much more Sarah really knew. Even

Donelli had been convinced she had been withholding evidence.

"Why do you think that?" she asked.

"She kept saying she was responsible."

"She told me that, too, but it didn't really make sense to me," Amanda said. "Did she tell you why?"

"Never in so many words. I'm sorry. I was hoping that when she'd had time to think about it, she would go to the police. She was a very caring, gentle woman. She would have done the right thing. I'm sure of it. Perhaps that's why she was killed, though it doesn't seem to fit in with my theory at all."

"If you have a theory, Mr. Rosen, tell us about it."

"But it's only a guess."

"That's okay. Every little bit helps."

Henry nodded. "Well, from things she said to me, I developed an impression that she had met someone since leaving New York, perhaps someone who had become quite important to her or wanted to become important. I wondered if, perhaps, it was not he who killed my brother."

CHAPTER

Thirteen

IT was a very long flight home.

Amanda was depressed by their failure to find conclusive evidence that would pin the murder either on Henry or, for that matter, on Tina. It seemed they were no further along in the investigation than they'd been on the very first day. They had suspects galore, but more questions than answers.

"Damn, this is frustrating," she finally said aloud. "I was so sure we were on the right track."

"Me, too." Donelli took her hand and rubbed his thumb across her knuckles. As a distraction, it was a reasonably effective gesture. Certainly it raised an entirely different line of thought, one with an equally unresolved outcome.

"I wish we could have stayed a little longer in New York," he said.

Amanda was surprised by the hint of longing in his voice. "I thought you hated it there."

"I never said I hated it, Amanda. I grew to hate living there. I hated feeling powerless to change things. But I do know why you love it so. I understand all about its frenetic personality and how it can get under your skin. I doubt if there's another city in America that's so alive, that offers so much."

"But you don't want to go back?"

"Not to live. New York is like a giant smorgasbord, filled to overflowing with things you want to sample. But it's not a meal for every day. Not for me, anyway. I would have liked to stay on this time, though, so we could have shared it. We could have seen a play, taken the Staten Island ferry, maybe gone to the Bronx Zoo and the Metropolitan Museum."

"You just hit on some of my favorite things."

"I know."

"How? Did you run another computer profile, Detective? I wasn't aware the FBI cared that much about my hobbies."

"Cute, Amanda. Actually I saw what you marked in the listings in the back of that magazine on the flight up. You didn't get to do any of them. You still miss it, don't you?"

Amanda hesitated, suddenly not at all sure what to answer. Her uncertainty surprised her. "Not as much somehow," she said finally. "It was all just the way I remembered it, but the feeling of excitement I had was all wrapped up in the pursuit of the story, not in the city. The last few weeks in Georgia have been different. I haven't felt as isolated or as totally useless."

"Then the case has helped you hold on to your sanity?"

She nodded, then regarded him with a bold directness. "You've helped, too."

"How?"

She grinned. "Now you're the one who wants to talk our rather unique relationship to death?"

"I think I'm beginning to see the importance of communication, yes."

"Or are you just hoping for a little flattery?"

"Perhaps that, too."

"Okay, maybe it's because until I met you, Georgia was all tied up with Mack and what happened between us. I hated the antebellum houses because Mack loved them. I disliked the countryside because Mack had taken me there and left me. I'm not saying I'm crazy about it now," she said, just in case he was getting any wild ideas. "But at least I realize I was blaming the place for what happened in my marriage, when it had nothing to do with that at all. If Mack was ready to meet someone, it could just as easily have happened at Columbia. New York might have a certain magic, but it's not a miracle worker. You gave me enough self-confidence to admit that."

"I've never thought of you as lacking in self-confidence."

"In some areas of my life, it's not a problem. I've always known what I wanted out of life. I worked damn hard to get where I was as a reporter. I was respected. I was in control. I always felt secure about my personal life, too, until Mack walked out. It was really the first thing to ever go really wrong for me. It shook me to see how easily that control could slip away."

"Do you still love him?"

She gave the question serious thought. "There are things about him I will always love," she admitted at last. "But I've let him go finally. Holding on to the emotions meant holding on to the pain. That hardly seems wise."

"We don't always do the wise thing when it comes to our feelings."

"You mean like you and me?"

Donelli nodded.

"We are very different," she agreed.

"Too different?"

She met his gaze evenly. "I hope not."

"Maybe it's not fair to ask you this now, but will you still go back to New York, if that call comes?"

Amanda had never been able to avoid honesty, not even when it hurt. "Maybe."

"Did you talk to *The Times*, while we were there?"

Gray eyes lifted to meet brown. She saw doubts in Donelli's eyes—doubts and fears, but she also saw the hope that comes with *maybe* instead of certainty.

"No," she said softly. "I didn't call. They know where to find me."

He nodded and a pleased smile played about his lips as he leaned back in his seat and closed his eyes. He didn't let go of her hand.

Amanda's nerves were on edge during the entire ride from Atlanta to her house. Donelli left the car and walked her to the door. When he drew her gently into his arms, she could feel his tension. Her head rested against his solid chest and his heart raced beneath her ear. When his fingers tangled in her hair and he tilted her face up for the touch of his lips, the warmth he had brought into her life exploded into raging fire. Yearning became desire. Doubts fled, replaced by certainty.

And still he let her go.

His eyes never left hers and they were filled with a raw, primitive excitement. "God, I want you," he said, holding her in a loose embrace, his hands resting lightly on her hips.

Amanda's breath caught in her throat, but she saw the regret in his expression and knew that no matter the depth of his need or hers, he would wait until love was as strong as hunger. Patience had never seemed less like a virtue.

"I should go," he said, his hands falling to his sides.

"You don't want to."

"No. I don't want to. But I should see Bobby Ray tonight, and tomorrow's going to be busy."

"Will I see you then?"

"I'll stop by for breakfast. Maybe we can put our heads together and come up with a few answers."

"Sounds promising," she said with a deliberate suggestiveness.

Donelli shook his head. "Good night, Amanda." He was whistling as he walked away.

Inside the house, Amanda found that she couldn't settle down. Finally she put on her robe, made herself a cup of tea, and sat down on the sofa with a notebook and pencil. Once more she made a list of the suspects, adding detail after detail beneath each name. Still nothing added up.

And what of Henry Rosen's theory that Sarah had met someone new? Was that significant? Was it even true?

Of course, if Henry Rosen had left Atlanta on Wednesday, then someone else had eaten that last dinner with her on the Friday night before she died.

Something tugged at her memory, playing cat and mouse with her conscious mind. Was it an offhand remark or something more specific?

Suddenly it came to her. Excitement flooded through her, followed by absolute certainty that she was right. She knew who killed Chef Maurice and why. But Donelli and Oscar would never believe her, not without solid evidence. All she had were circumstantial tidbits and suspicions, but she knew exactly where to go to start building the case. She would begin in the morning.

The first thing Amanda had to do was avoid Donelli. She was up at dawn, showered and dressed by seven. She left a note on the door explaining that she was on an unexpected assignment and would meet him at the newspaper office at noon.

She stopped at a doughnut shop in town and ordered her usual—coffee and a huge blueberry muffin to go.

"You're up mighty early, Amanda," Virginia Beatty said as she poured the coffee. "We don't usually see you until after nine. You're in luck, too. The muffins just came out of the oven."

"Terrific. Maybe I should take two. I missed dinner last night."

"I heard you went up to New York. I didn't think Oscar was expecting you back quite so soon."

"He wasn't, but our lead didn't pan out quite the way we expected. We took a late flight last night."

"You and Joe seem to be getting along real well. He's

a handsome guy. Nice, too. You two ought to have a lot in common, both of you coming from New York and all."

Amanda thought of all the things they didn't have in common, beginning with that awful music Donelli liked. There was also her impulsiveness countered by his plodding patience. Still, she had to admit the man had possibilities. Maybe he could wear earphones when he listened to the music. Maybe a man like Donelli needed someone like her to shake up his tame existence.

Virginia was leaning against the counter waiting for a response. Amanda knew whatever she said would be served up to the day's customers along with the coffee, doughnuts, and freshly-baked muffins.

"We've had to do some work together lately, Virginia. Don't make too much out of that," she said, taking her order and leaving. The bell over the door chimed as she left.

She drove to a park on the outskirts of town, parked, and ate the muffin. As she sipped the coffee, she tried to plan the questions she would ask. Like talking to Virginia, this particular interview would require discretion.

When she finally drove up to Miss Martha's, the front door was still closed and the drapes were drawn, but she could see that the elderly woman was on the side porch having her breakfast.

When Della answered the door, Amanda said, "I'm sorry to drop by so early. Do you think Miss Wellington would be willing to see me, Della? It's important."

"Who is it, Della?" Miss Martha was already partway into the living room. She was dressed for the day and every white hair was in place. "Why, Amanda, dear. How delightful. Come join me for a cup of coffee. Would you like breakfast? Della could fix you something."

"No, thank you, Miss Martha. I just wondered if we could talk for a few minutes."

"Certainly, dear. Come with me."

When they were seated on the porch and Della had brought another cup and a fresh pot of coffee, Miss Martha regarded her curiously. "Now what brings you out to see an old woman like me this early in the day?"

"When I was here the other day, you said something. I've been thinking about it and I wondered exactly what you meant. You said you knew Sarah Robbins."

"Why, certainly. Does this have anything to do with her death?"

"I'm not sure yet, but it could have. Did you meet her when she began to work for Bobby Ray?"

"Yes. I believe she'd just been in town a few weeks."

"You said Bobby Ray brought her by here."

"He certainly did. I thought it was a lovely thing to do. She was a newcomer, after all, and it was just good business on his part to see that she knew the ladies who'd be shopping at that store of his."

"Had he ever done that before?"

Miss Martha appeared puzzled by the question. "No, but I don't believe there was ever any need before that. Most of the clerks he hired had lived around here all their lives. Sarah was someone new and you know how small towns can be. Folks can be real standoffish until they get to know you. I'm sure you've experienced some of that yourself."

"I suppose at first, but you've all made me feel very welcome, especially since I started working for the paper."

"I'm glad, child. It's good for us to have some new blood around this old town. Much as I love it, it can get a little boring seeing the same people day in and day out your whole life."

"I'm sure it does. Miss Martha, when Bobby Ray and Sarah were here, did it seem to you that they might have been more than boss and employee?"

Miss Martha's eyes lit up at the hint of romance. "You know, I wondered about that. Bobby Ray certainly did seem smitten. He's been very much alone since his wife died a few years back. I was rather hoping that something would come of that interest he seemed to be showing in Sarah."

"But it didn't?"

"Not that I know of, dear. I asked him about her a few times after that, but he didn't say too much. I got the feeling she must have cared for someone else."

"I know this must seem like a strange thing to ask, but what was Bobby Ray's marriage like? Were they happy?"

"As far as anyone around here knew. Janie was a pretty little thing, not as sophisticated as Sarah, but just as attractive. She had a lot of beaus before she married Bobby Ray."

"Did that bother him?"

"I don't know why it should have." Her brow knit in

a frown. "But, now that you ask me, I do believe I heard once that Bobby Ray was the jealous type. I don't think Janie ever did' anything to provoke it, but with some men that doesn't seem to matter."

Amanda sat back at last and took a long sip of the delicious coffee. She felt triumphant. The pieces were beginning to fit. She had the motive. All she needed was opportunity. It was just possible that Larry's original photos might contain what she needed.

She got to her feet. "Miss Martha, you've been wonderful. I'm terribly sorry for barging in here so early."

"Don't you dare apologize. I loved having the company. I hope I was able to give you the help you needed. You come back again whenever you like, dear."

"You were a tremendous help. Don't get up. I'll show myself out."

Amanda drove directly to the newspaper office. It was still locked up. Oscar usually didn't come in until ten. Amanda unlocked the door and went straight to Oscar's desk. She used her duplicate key to open the lap drawer and take out the pictures. Using a magnifying glass to study the tiny prints, she finally found what she wanted on the roll Larry had shot when they first arrived at the store. There was no crowd yet, just a scattering of employees and one person at the demonstration table.

With a whoop of triumph, she picked up the phone to call Donelli. She never heard the movement of the darkroom door. Nor did she feel the presence of another person creeping soundlessly up behind her. It was only at the last instant that she sensed the danger and by then it was too late. Something cold and hard hit the side of her head and then she was hurtling into darkness.

Amanda awoke to the by-now familiar sound of Donelli's muttered curses. He was patting her cheeks... perhaps with a little more force than necessary.

"You've been wanting to do that for days now, haven't you?" she mumbled groggily, peering at him out of the one eye it didn't hurt to open.

"What happened?"

"Don't you know any other questions? That one's getting a bit repetitious."

"Tell me about it," he said dryly. "Is there a new variation on the answer?"

"Would you believe I fell down in the bathroom and hit my head on the edge of the sink?"

"I might, if you can tell me how you got from there to your office."

She tried to sit up and groaned as pretty-colored lights danced before her eyes. "I'll have to think about that while I'm recuperating."

Donelli pressed a cool cloth against the back of her head. She closed her eyes and enjoyed the sensation of having him take care of her. "That feels good, Donelli."

"I'm glad. Now try to tell me what happened."

"I spent the morning checking out a lead. It paid off. I came back here to look at Larry's contact sheets again, just to be sure."

"Did you find what you were looking for?"

"Yes. It was plain as day. I don't know why we didn't figure it out before."

"Amanda, are you enjoying dragging this out? Do you know who the killer is or not?"

"I know." She tried very hard not to look smug. Then she hesitated and chewed on her lower lip. "You're not going to like it."

"I will only hate it if you did it. Just tell me."

"Bobby Ray."

CHAPTER

Fourteen

"**B**OBBY Ray Johnson?"

Donelli's incredulous hoot no doubt could be heard clear to Atlanta. Amanda held her aching head and glared at him.

"I think that blow to your head scrambled your brains." He regarded her closely, as if looking for additional signs of damage.

"Don't look at me like that," she said with a sniff. "I told you you weren't going to like it. But if you would just stop and think about it objectively for a minute, it makes perfect sense."

"Amanda, Bobby Ray hired me to find the killer," Donelli reminded her. He sounded like a man whose patience was being tested. He also sounded tolerant, which was worse.

"Do you think he would have done that if he were guilty?" he asked.

"Why not?" she insisted stubbornly. "It certainly

threw the suspicion off him. He had you looking every which way but right here in your own backyard. The only thing that surprises me is that he didn't force you to pick a likely candidate from among the suspects and then go out and make an arrest so he could wrap the whole thing up."

Donelli looked decidedly uncomfortable at that. She studied him suspiciously. "Did you see him last night?"

"Yes."

"What happened?"

Donelli sighed. "He told me that since all the evidence clearly pointed toward Jean-Claude, he was going to arrest him today. He's closing the case."

Amanda was horrified. "Dammit, Donelli, we can't let him do that." She struggled to her feet and clung to the desk, waiting for a wave of nausea and dizziness to pass.

"Amanda, sit down. You're in no condition to go racing all over the countryside."

"I am not going to let Bobby Ray Johnson arrest an innocent man just so he can get away with murder." Yelling at Donelli took the last of her strength and she sagged against the desk.

Donelli pushed a chair under her. "Oh, for heaven's sake," he snapped as he did it. "If you're so damn sure of yourself, I'll go and try to stop him."

"Then you do believe me?"

"I didn't say that, but I do agree it's too soon for an arrest. I'll try one more time to convince Bobby Ray of that. Will that satisfy you?"

"Almost. I'm going with you."

"You are not going anywhere, except possibly to a doctor's office to get that head wound checked out."

"My head is perfectly fine, thank you very much. If you don't let me go with you, I'll just follow in my car and I'm certainly in less condition to drive than I am to ride."

"Oh . . ." He stumbled over the expletive he clearly wanted to use. "Oh, for crying out loud!"

Amanda chuckled. "I'm impressed by your restraint, Donelli."

"Be thankful someone already knocked you out or I'd be tempted to do it myself," he muttered. "I suppose you think that was Bobby Ray, too."

"If the contact sheets are missing, I can practically guarantee it."

Donelli looked at the top of Oscar's desk. "They're here."

"All of them?"

He picked them up and began counting. "How many should there be?"

"Twelve," she said just as Donelli said "Eleven." She could tell from his voice it was the last one in his hand.

"One's missing," he said as if he couldn't quite believe it.

"The one Larry shot before the demonstration began," Amanda guessed. Thumbing through them, she confirmed it.

"Why that one?"

"It was shot before the crowd arrived. It has an interesting photo of the stage. Bobby Ray is right in the middle of it. We overlooked it before because what would be more natural than the store manager checking things out before the big event?"

"Oh, hell."

"Exactly. Now do you believe me?"

"What you've told me so far is hardly conclusive, but as much as I regret it, I'm beginning to think you could be right. I suppose you have the motive all figured out, too."

She nodded. "He was in love with Sarah."

Donelli's brows lifted incredulously. "How in the devil did you come up with that?"

"Miss Martha. She mentioned the other day that Bobby Ray had brought Sarah over to the house once. I stopped by there this morning and she confirmed that it appeared Bobby Ray had more than a supervisory interest in his sales clerk. She also mentioned something else rather interesting."

"What's that?"

"Bobby Ray has a past history of jealousy. He was very possessive about his wife, too. That all fits in with what Henry Rosen told us, don't you think?"

"Yes," he conceded reluctantly, then sighed. "I really hate this."

Amanda touched his cheek. "I know you do. I'm sorry."

"Well, there's no point in being sorry. Let's go after him and see what he has to say."

They were all the way into downtown Atlanta before Donelli asked, "Amanda, what about Sarah? Surely you don't think he would have killed her if he was in love with her."

"I'm not sure what to make of that. Miss Martha

didn't say anything about him being violent, but I suppose it fits the pattern in extreme cases of jealousy. I guess we won't know for sure, though, until we talk to him. Unless . . ."

"Unless what?"

"Unless the Atlanta police have evidence that it was Bobby Ray who ate that last meal with Sarah."

Donelli smacked the palm of his hand against the steering wheel. "Damn!"

"What?"

"They did find his fingerprints in her place, but they paid no attention to it because he was the one who found her. In fact, the cops in Atlanta were laughing about it. They thought it was a hoot that the small-time sheriff didn't know any better than to keep his hands off things at a crime scene."

Amanda regarded him solemnly. "That just about clinches it, doesn't it?"

"Looks that way."

When they arrived at the hotel a few minutes later, they found Jean-Claude in his room packing. Since he was doing it neatly, it didn't appear he was rushing to get out of town to escape an arrest warrant.

"Mr. Donelli, Miss Roberts, do come in. As you can see, I am getting ready to leave for the next stop on my tour. I hope I have your permission."

"Has the sheriff been by to see you yet?" Donelli asked.

"Why, no. Was he planning to stop by to ask more questions?"

"He was planning to arrest you."

That shook Jean-Claude's calm demeanor. Color rose

in his cheeks and he demanded, "On what charge? I have done nothing, unless you consider it a crime to overcook the asparagus I prepared for my class this week."

"He was going to charge you with killing Chef Maurice and, quite likely, attempt to get you indicted for the death of Sarah Robbins as well."

Thoroughly alarmed now, he shouted, "This is absurd! A travesty! I will call my lawyer and have him fly down immediately."

Amanda put a hand on his arm. "I don't think that will be necessary, Jean-Claude. He is only trying to cast the blame away from himself."

Jean-Claude sank down on the edge of the bed, still holding a pair of socks. "This sheriff, he killed Maurice?"

"We believe so. We thought he might be arresting you today and we came to try and stop him." She looked at Donelli. "Why hasn't he been here already?"

"I have one idea."

A thought struck Amanda at the same instant. "Sarah's?"

"Could be. Let's check it out."

"And what should I do?" Jean-Claude asked. "Must I remain here and wait for this imbecile to come?"

"I don't believe that's necessary," Donelli said. "Can you give us a copy of your itinerary?"

"Certainly." He pulled a sheet of paper from a folder in his luggage.

Donelli folded the schedule and tucked it in his pocket. "Okay, Amanda. Let's go."

Amanda paused at the door. "Good-bye, Jean-Claude. I'm sorry we had to meet under these circumstances."

"As am I, mademoiselle. Perhaps I shall come back one day and we can discuss French cooking in more depth."

"I would like that."

"*Au revoir*, then."

When they were back in the car, Donelli kept glancing at Amanda. "Are you okay?"

"Fine."

"Then why do you keep rubbing your head?"

"It hurts some, that's all."

"How much is some?"

"Dammit, Donelli. I was whacked over the head. How do you expect it to feel?"

"I'm taking you to a hospital."

"I am not going to any hospital. Will you just get over to Sarah's apartment? My head will feel a whole lot better, if we stop arguing."

Donelli's sigh was particularly heavy and long-suffering.

Despite all her brave talk, Amanda was still slow to get out of the car when they reached Sarah's. Donelli looked at her sharply and his lips drew into a tight line, but he didn't say a word. She had a hunch it was killing him.

"If he's here, maybe I should go in and try to talk to him," she suggested.

"Are you out of your mind? If you're right about Bobby Ray, then he's already tried to kill you twice. Do you want to give him another chance?"

"I don't think he wants to kill me," she said confidently.

"And exactly how did you come to this brilliant conclusion?"

"It's perfectly obvious, if you stop to think about it."

"I don't have time to deal with your particularly circuitous logic. Enlighten me."

"Bobby Ray is a hunter, right?"

"He goes deer hunting, which, if you don't mind my saying so, seems rather far afield from what we're talking about."

"Not at all. Since he hunts, presumably with reasonable success, don't you think he could have hit me when he shot at the car? He shot twice before I went off the road. After that, it would have been even easier. I was a sitting target, but there was no third shot." She paused before adding the coup de grace, "Because he didn't want to kill me, just scare me."

"I suppose in a twisted sort of way that makes sense," Donelli admitted reluctantly.

"Make all the cracks you like about my thought process, you can't deny the obvious. Even today, he didn't kill me. He only knocked me out."

"Fine. I concede you might have a point. That still doesn't mean that I am about to let you go into that apartment alone. He might not have killed you before, but if you start hitting him with your guesswork, he just might decide he's made a mistake leaving you on the loose."

"Okay. Terrific. Let's just go, before he escapes out the backdoor."

"Amanda, there is no backdoor."

"Back window, then. Stop stalling, Donelli."

Donelli did seem to be amazingly reluctant to go after Bobby Ray. Amanda wasn't sure if he simply hated the thought of arresting a friend or if he was worried about her getting hurt in the cross fire. It was also possible that even at this late date, he still had doubts about Bobby Ray's guilt.

After what seemed an interminable wait, he nodded and continued up the walk. He approached the door of Sarah's apartment cautiously and was just about to try the knob when it swung open.

"I was wondering how long it would take you to get here," Bobby Ray said. He was holding a gun in his hand. Because he wasn't pointing it at them, Amanda ignored it. Donelli, however, tensed beside her. Bobby Ray used the gun to motion for them to come in.

He looked like hell, she thought, even worse than he had when Amanda had last seen him with Tina White-head in Atlanta. His complexion was gray beneath his tan, and his eyes reflected an incredible pain. He turned and walked back into the apartment. He dropped down into the nearest chair, put the gun down beside him, and buried his face in his hands.

Donelli visibly relaxed. His hand, which she was certain had been very close to reaching for his concealed gun, dropped to his side.

"I'm real sorry, boy," Bobby Ray murmured. "I shouldn't have gotten you mixed up in this."

"Why did you?" Donelli asked quietly. "You could have handled the whole thing yourself and there's a good chance no one would ever have figured it out."

Bobby Ray looked up for a moment. "I guess maybe I wanted to get caught, leastways that's probably what some psychologist would say. I figured you were the best man to do it. It's funny, though, after a few days, I began to think maybe everything would be okay. You had all these other suspects and I figured you could make a tidy case against one of them. Looked like lots of folks besides me wanted to get the guy."

"Maybe if I'd only relied on circumstantial evidence, that's what would have happened," Donelli conceded. "But every time I got close, I kept bumping into something that didn't quite hang together."

"Still, I began to think, 'Hey, maybe it's going to be all right. Maybe you'll get away with it, Bobby Ray.' What made you finally figure out it was me, Joe?"

"I didn't. It was Amanda who put all the pieces together. She'd make a helluva cop."

Bobby Ray managed a weary smile. "You were slow picking up on that, too, weren't you, boy? I knew the minute I met her she had the kind of mind it takes to work out a puzzle like this. She's got tenacity, too. It's a mighty powerful combination. Watch out for her, son. She'll give you a run for it if you ever decide to get back into this business for good."

Donelli glanced over at Amanda. "I don't doubt it for a minute. Is that why you tried to kill her? Because you guessed she was on to you?"

Bobby Ray scowled at him. "Hell, boy, I didn't try to kill her. If I'd been trying, do you think she'd be sitting here with us now?"

Amanda shot a triumphant look at Donelli.

"Don't say it," he warned.

"Why not? You rub it in when you're right." She looked at Bobby Ray and suddenly felt sorry for him.

He looked like a man who'd lost everything and, worse, knew it was his own fault. "What really happened, Bobby Ray?"

"Maybe you're the one who should be telling me."

She smiled at the tribute. "I have some ideas, but I'd like to hear it from you."

He closed his eyes and leaned back. When he opened them again, it was as though he were looking at some distant place.

"A few months back, Sarah came into the store looking for a job. You saw her. She was a mighty good-looking woman. Pretty as a picture. Had a head on her shoulders, too. I took her to lunch the day she applied for the job and we seemed to hit it off."

He smiled then and his expression softened. "I saw her a few times after that. Every time, I don't know, it just seemed to get more special to me. Pretty soon I knew I was crazy about her, but she was holding back like. Finally, I asked her about it. She told me she'd been hurt real bad by this man up North. She said the scars were pretty deep, that she thought it would be a long time before she could make another commitment."

"How did you feel about that?" Amanda asked.

"I told her I'd wait and I would have, too. I'd have waited for however long it took, but then the guy came to town or rather she got him there. I didn't know he was the one at first, not when she came to me about having this hotshot chef do a demonstration. I thought it sounded like a terrific idea and I could tell she was excited about it. Why, those eyes of hers just twinkled like stars every time she talked about it. It was the first time she'd seemed really happy since I'd met her."

"When did you find out Chef Maurice was the man she'd been involved with?"

"Wasn't 'til the night before the demonstration. She was in a real tizzy, wanting things to be just so. I stopped by her place after work, just to give her a few reassuring words, you know. She was sitting in here crying her eyes out"

"Did she tell you what was wrong?"

"She told me all about it. She told me about how he'd dumped her in New York, how he'd stolen recipes from his brother and gotten all mixed up with this high-class public relations lady. That wasn't what had her so upset, though. He'd just been here. He'd told her he was going to marry that other lady. He said he'd never stopped loving her, but the Whitehead woman was his future. I mean to tell you, it just about broke my heart listening to her. I ain't never seen anybody torn up like that, 'cept maybe me after Janie died. Damn, it made me angry."

"So you decided to kill him for Sarah's sake," Amanda said softly. She was glad, somehow, that it hadn't happened in a jealous rage.

Bobby Ray looked at her, tears in his eyes. "It don't make no sense hearing you say it now, but that's what I was thinking all right. It wasn't until after it was too late that I saw what I had done. I hadn't just killed that chef. I'd killed any chance of Sarah ever loving me back."

"Did you kill Sarah, Bobby Ray?" It was Donelli who asked the question Amanda had been afraid to put into words.

The man broke down then, his sobs horrible to hear in the room's heavy silence. "I didn't kill her, not the way you mean. I couldn't have done that. She was the only thing in my life that meant anything."

"But if you didn't . . ."

"Don't you see yet? I might as well have. Like the note said, Sarah killed herself."

"Are you absolutely sure of that?"

"As sure as I can be without having been right here beside her. I'd been over here the night before. She asked me point-blank if I'd killed that Chef Maurice. I couldn't lie to her. Weren't no point to it anyway. She already knew. She didn't say another word after that. It was like she was already gone. I was real worried about her, so I came back the next morning. That's when I found her."

He stared at Amanda. "You know the worst part? I think maybe she could have lived with that man out of her life for good. She probably could have picked up the pieces and gone on. But she couldn't live with knowing what I'd done to him. She felt responsible."

There it was again, Amanda thought. Poor Sarah's burden of responsibility, her conviction that even though Bobby Ray had put the cyanide within Chef Maurice's grasp, it was she who'd led him to do it.

"I thought you were coming into town today to arrest Jean-Claude," Donelli said. "What stopped you?"

"I got as far as the hotel, but I couldn't do it. Near as I could tell, I was already guilty in two deaths. I didn't want ruining another life on my conscience."

"We're going to have to turn you in, Bobby Ray," Donelli said.

"I know that."

"I feel terrible about it."

"Don't go feeling bad on my account, boy. It's the right thing to do. I'm not looking forward to jail, but this is one debt I aim to pay."

Delivering Bobby Ray to the authorities and waiting until his attorney arrived to be with him took Donelli and Amanda the rest of the afternoon. As soon as Donelli gave his report to the police, he made calls to Jonathan Webster and Tina Whitehead to give them the news and to tell them they were free to leave town.

When they were on their way home at last, Donelli said, "Well, that's done now."

"Not quite," Amanda said. "I still have to write my story. Drop me at the paper, would you?"

"Amanda, you ought to be going home and getting some rest."

"I'll rest later. I want to write it while everything is still fresh in my mind."

"How do you think Oscar's going to handle the news? He and Bobby Ray were friends, too. They grew up together."

Amanda imagined the lurid headlines Oscar could have come up with for the story had the killer been anyone other than Bobby Ray. The fact that the murder had been committed by someone local would tame his desire for sensationalism.

"I think he'll treat him fairly," she said.

"And you?"

"Do you even need to ask? I'm not out to crucify anyone, Donelli. I just want to report the news."

"And then?"

She knew what he meant. "I'll get to work on the next assignment."

"Here?" he persisted.

"That depends."

"On what?"

"If I have another offer, if Oscar still wants me around, you."

"Me?" His expression brightened.

Amanda laughed and warned, "Don't push it, Donelli. This could still go either way."

CHAPTER

Fifteen

IF Oscar was distraught about what his longtime friend Bobby Ray had done, he hid it behind a convincing facade of enthusiasm for Amanda's in-depth story. He even told her to make it as long as she liked.

"If I have to kill one or two of them regular columns, it won't hurt nothing," he said. Because he considered those round ups of social activities and gardening tips to be sacrosanct, it was quite a concession.

"Damn, this is good," he said, peering over her shoulder and ripping each page out of the typewriter as she finished it. Having Oscar breathing down her neck as she wrote was one thing. His ongoing commentary was quite another. She was only human. She couldn't help basking in the praise.

"Hell of a story, girl. Hell of a story. Can't wait to show it to Wiley and Larry. They're going to be real proud of you, too. We're gonna enter this one for some of those big prizes. Maybe not a Pulitzer, but they got journalism contests in Atlanta. This is better than anything I've seen in those papers over there."

Amanda tried to rein him in. "I'm glad you like it, Oscar, but it's not exactly like doing a major exposé on civic corruption."

"Girl, this is solid reporting. The best. That's what counts. You've got all your facts. You're objective, but you can feel Bobby Ray's pain in this story. You can understand what he did. I gotta thank you for that."

Oscar's delight was rewarding, but Amanda felt she had to caution him. "There are going to be people in town who won't like it, Oscar. Bobby Ray is a popular man. Some folks may even blame us for doing a story at all. They'd prefer to read about the quilting circles and pie-eating contest. You make 'em nervous when you shake their complacency."

"Then that's their problem," he said staunchly. "I'm not running this paper to whitewash anybody. Bobby Ray committed a crime. It's up to us to say he did. If the folks around here can't live with that, then it's just too bad."

By late the next afternoon, the *Gazette* was embroiled in the controversy Amanda had predicted. The town seemed split between those who supported the paper's detailed, if sympathetic, story and those who thought it was a low blow aimed at a favorite son right when he was down. The phones rang off the hook. Finally they assigned old Wiley the task of answering them. He turned down the volume on his hearing aid to do it. One call, though, he insisted Amanda take.

"Miss Roberts, this is Joel Crenshaw. I'm with *Inside Atlanta* magazine."

"I'm sorry, Mr. Crenshaw. I'm not familiar with it."

"Of course you're not. It's new. We won't put our first issue out for another six months. A friend of mine told me about that story you broke today about Chef Maurice's murder. I was wondering if we could talk."

"Are you interested in a free-lance article?"

"Actually, no. I have an opening here for a staff writer. I need somebody who knows how to dig behind the scenes and do some hard-hitting reporting. Are you interested?"

Amanda hesitated. It would mean making a commitment to Georgia. It would also mean giving her relationship with Donelli the time it needed to develop. "I'd like to hear what you have to say."

"That's fantastic. When can we meet?"

"You name the time and place."

He suggested a restaurant in Atlanta for the following day. "By the way, you don't happen to know any good editors, do you? I know how to put a magazine like this together, but I don't know much about the day-to-day operation, developing assignments, that sort of thing."

"I think I might know someone," she said, glancing at Oscar. "I'll have to talk to him about it first, though."

"Terrific. You can tell me about him when we meet."

How would she explain about Oscar, she wondered as she hung up. How did you describe a man who came alive at the prospect of a big story? How did you explain that lurking under a tough, chauvinistic exterior were the quick mind and intuitive senses of a solid, dependable journalist? How did you explain that you'd misjudged him for months because of your own subtle biases?

"Damn. I haven't had this much fun in years," Oscar gloated, throwing an arm around her. "This is just the kind of newspapering I always dreamed about."

Suddenly he was behaving as if hiring Amanda was just the beginning of some grand scheme he had for her and his paper.

"You keep this up, you can take over the paper one day, if you want to," he promised. "I ain't got no sons to leave it to. I'd be proud to see your name on the masthead."

Amanda was astounded by the impulsive statement. "Oscar, it's too soon to be talking like that. You're not going to be retiring for years yet."

"Oh, I might start taking it a little easier, if I know you're around to handle things."

"Oscar, you'll go just as nuts as I do if you start taking it easy. Who are you trying to kid?"

"I guess what I'm trying to say is I don't want to lose you. I know you can do better someplace else, but selfishly I want you to stay right here. As usual, I'm probably making a mess of saying it."

"No, you're not. I appreciate the offer more than you can possibly know, but this may not be the right place for me. I've just been talking to a new magazine in Atlanta. They're looking for someone to do some investigative reporting on what's going on in the area."

His face fell. "Are you going to take it?"

"There's no offer yet."

"I'd like to tell you I'll match whatever they offer, but, even if I had it, it's not the money that matters to you, is it?"

She shook her head. "It's the challenge. I just want to

see what direction they're planning for the magazine. Even if I like what I hear, there are a couple of things I need to work out before I make a final decision."

"Donelli wouldn't happen to be one of them, would he?"

"If he were, I wouldn't tell you, Oscar. You'd print it on the front page of this week's edition."

"I most certainly would not," he said indignantly. "As long as you promise me an exclusive, I won't break the embargo on the story and run it before you say I can."

"There's nothing to report. If and when there is, you'll be the first to know."

"Where are you going?" he asked as she picked up her purse and a handful of jelly beans.

"Shopping." She started out the door. "By the way, the publisher of that magazine in Atlanta asked me if I knew any good editors who might be interested in a job. Should I give 'em your name?"

Now he was the one who looked surprised and pleased. "You'd do that for me?"

"I think it might be about time for you to take a crack at the big time, Oscar. Think about it. You wouldn't even have to move."

No matter what happened, Amanda knew she'd never forget the smile on Oscar's face when she left him to think about the prospect of taking on something bigger than the *Gazette*.

Nor was she ever likely to forget the flash of fire in Donelli's eyes when he came charging up to her in the lingerie department at the Johnson and Watkins Superstore a half hour later.

"What's this I hear about you leaving town?"

"Who said anything about my leaving?" She held up a negligee. "What do you think?"

"Oscar's just been telling me about some big magazine offer. He's convinced you're going to take it. How the hell can you do something like that without even mentioning it to me?"

He yanked the seductive black negligee out of her hands and put it back on the rack. He shoved a pink one into her hands. "The other one'll make you look like a hooker."

Amanda fought to control a grin. "Are you sure you wouldn't like me to model them for you before you make a decision like that."

He stared at her. "What are you trying to do to me?"

"What am I trying to do to you?" she repeated. "If it's not obvious by now, you're not half the cop I thought you were."

"Fine. Great. You want to seduce me and then go running off to some new job. I hate to say it, Amanda, but you have a really rotten idea of what it takes to make a relationship work."

"I think I have a pretty good idea, as a matter of fact." She put back the other negligee and took Donelli by the hand.

"Where are we going?"

"To my house to finish this conversation."

He stopped in his tracks. "Not a good idea."

She shrugged. "We can finish it here, but you're going to hate the publicity."

He glanced around and noticed they were beginning to draw a crowd. "Come on, Amanda," he growled. She tried very hard not to grin.

It was much later when they got around to talking again.

"Amanda, you are the most infuriating, reckless, contradictory woman I have ever known."

Because he was running a hand along the bare curve of her hip when he said it, she didn't take the comment too seriously. "You're just mad because I caught on to Bobby Ray before you did."

"I am mad because one minute you're in bed with me and the next you're considering packing up and moving without even discussing it with me."

"Who said anything about moving?"

"Oscar did."

"Are you sure?"

"He said you'd had a job offer from a big magazine."

"That's true."

"Big magazines are in New York."

"For a man who dedicated his life to gathering evidence, you can sometimes miss what's staring you right in the face."

"Amanda, would you stop talking in riddles?"

"Certainly. The magazine is in Atlanta. I would not have to move, therefore I saw no need to rush out and tell you about it before I even meet with the guy. Actually, I thought you'd be pleased to hear I'm thinking of staying."

"I am." Then he frowned. "Why haven't you decided yet?"

"I was more interested in finding a sexy negligee."

"As you may have noticed, you didn't need it."

"Donelli, romance is just as important as sex."

"Okay. Wear the negligee next time, if it'll make you happy."

"The point is to make you happy. Why should I spend a hundred dollars on some flimsy piece of material if you're not even going to look at it?"

He blinked at her instantaneous reversal. "God, the way your mind works terrifies me. I never, ever want to work with you again. You'll get yourself killed using that kind of logic."

"Does that mean you're considering Bobby Ray's idea?"

"What idea was that?"

"His suggestion that you get back to work as a detective."

"No way. I've left my tomatoes on their own for too long as it is."

She ran her fingers provocatively down his chest. "Then I don't suppose you want to hear about this fascinating jewel theft somebody tipped me off about. Some old family heirloom that's worth a fortune. Actually Larry heard about it while he was in the hospital."

"Amanda!"

"Rumor has it there's a ring in Atlanta that preys on wealthy widows and divorcées. I personally think that's a really lousy kind of scam. I mean what kind of a rotten person would take advantage of some grieving widow or vulnerable divorcée? Do you know, the last time the victim disappeared along with the jewelry. Fascinating, huh?"

Donelli didn't comment as she tugged absentmindedly at the hairs on his chest.

"I already have some ideas about how I can find out

what's going on," she said. "I was thinking of setting myself up as a divorcée, maybe getting some copies of really expensive jewels made. What do you think?"

"Amanda! Don't you dare!" he thundered. She could feel his heart begin to race beneath her fingers. She doubted it was from her touch. She got the distinct impression he wasn't wild about her plan.

"That's okay," she said cheerfully. "If you don't want to get involved, I'll handle it alone. It's going to be a terrific story."

"Amanda!"

"Good night, Donelli."